A Candlelight Ecstasy Romance™

SHE HEARD THE SOFT RUSTLE OF HER SILK DRESS AS HIS HANDS CARESSED HER. . . .

"I think I'd better be going," she managed hesitantly. But he ignored her words, taking advantage of her parted lips to abruptly deepen the kiss. She felt his seductive assault and trembled, knowing the small movement had communicated itself to him by the way he shifted his hold to mold her ever more closely to him.

Without thinking, Kendra lifted her hands to the darkness of his hair. He pulled back from her mouth and began a trail of tiny glowing kisses along the line of her cheek.

"Don't you realize," he whispered, "that every question you answer only raises a thousand more?"

AFFAIR OF RISK

Jayne Castle

A CANDLELIGHT ECSTASY ROMANCE™

Published by
Dell Publishing Co., Inc.
1 Dag Hammarskjold Plaza
New York, New York 10017

Dell ® TM 681510, Dell Publishing Co., Inc.

Candlelight Ecstasy Romance™ is a trademark of
Dell Publishing Co., Inc., New York, New York.

ISBN: 0-440-10054-2

Printed in the United States of America
First printing—May 1982

Dear Reader:

In response to your continued enthusiasm for Candlelight Ecstasy Romances™, we are increasing the number of new titles from four to six per month.

We are delighted to present sensuous novels set in America, depicting modern American men and women as they confront the provocative problems of modern relationships.

Throughout the history of the Candlelight line, Dell has tried to maintain a high standard of excellence to give you the finest in reading enjoyment. That is and will remain our most ardent ambition.

Anne Gisonny
Editor
Candlelight Romances

AFFAIR OF RISK

CHAPTER ONE

The crystal chandeliers threw a rich, glittering light over the elegant scene, and Kendra Loring paused on the marble steps above the thickly carpeted gambling floor to absorb it.

Her hand lifted absently to push back the white mink collar which framed her intent features and protected her against the snowy cold of the Lake Tahoe evening. For a moment her well-shaped, long nails, gleaming with the latest shade of expensive-looking red, sank into the thickness of the fur, creating a brilliant contrast. Then, with a deft movement, she let the collar fall once again to lay flat against the belted white mink coat.

Her cool hazel eyes flickered across the tables presided over by croupiers dressed in evening clothes as impeccable as those of the customers. Or did one refer to those who came to gamble as "customers" in a place as posh as this? Kendra wondered with a wry smile.

At this very intimate, very exclusive casino on the California-Nevada border, there were no flashing neon signs outside, no casually dressed, touristy patrons, and there was no harsh rattle of slot machines. Case Garrett's club had an old-world Monte Carlo sophistication about it.

A great deal of money had been lavished in an effort to reassure the wealthy crowd that they were indeed enjoying the leading edge of aristocratic entertainment. The casino was small, but the amount of money its clients dropped at the tables was not. Kendra had proof of that tucked inside the zipper pocket of the white mink muff she held in one hand.

The thought of that proof hardened the momentary humor that had touched her mouth as she considered the scene in front of her. She was here on business, and the sooner she concluded it, the better.

"Madam wishes to take a place at the baccarat table? Or perhaps the roulette wheel?" The voice was haughty and male; the accent fake French.

Kendra turned her head in surprise to find a large man in black-and-white evening dress standing politely at her side. There was a hint of a paunch not entirely concealed by the tailoring of his jacket, and the shoulders were much too wide. He was somewhere in his late thirties, she decided, assessing the once-broken nose and the watchful brown eyes. A well-dressed bouncer. And the fake French irritated her.

"*Mais, oui,*" she murmured in her best college French. "But later, perhaps. I am here to see Monsieur Garrett. Would you be so kind as to take me to him?"

She waited politely, knowing he hadn't understood a word she had said, and wondered if the phony accent would still be in place when he figured out an answer. But she was wrong. The man had caught one word and seized on it with obvious relief.

"Mister Garrett?" he said, gamely maintaining the accent and struggling to hold the haughty look. "You wish to see the owner?"

Again, driven by a perverse desire to destroy some of the expensive illusion around her, Kendra replied in French.

"If you would take me to him, I would be most grateful. He and I have business to transact, you understand." She lifted one eyebrow, affecting an expression every bit as arrogant as the bouncer's.

10

For a moment there was a war of wills conducted on the marble steps. Kendra knew she wasn't playing the game the way the man was accustomed to having it played. He had, in effect, politely asked her to identify herself, and she had failed to take the hint.

Her cool hazel eyes duelled with his narrowing gaze for a tense moment, and then she smiled in spite of herself. This time she spoke in English.

"If you'll just direct me to Mr. Garrett's office, I promise not to use any more school French on you. I'm not here to gamble. I have business with the casino owner."

The large man stared at her for an instant, and then a slow, unwilling smile crossed the somewhat scarred lips.

"I'd appreciate that, ma'am," he said in a flawless, perfectly natural longshoreman's drawl. "I didn't understand a word you said. Other than an Arab now and then, we don't get many folks who actually speak French."

"I'm sure your accent is most impressive in the majority of cases," she assured him coolly, her humor fading as she realized exactly who or what she might be conversing with. Even in evening dress, a bouncer was still a bouncer, and this man looked as if he had come to his present position after an extensive apprenticeship. She didn't care to dwell on the sort of tasks he might have performed during the long road to his current success.

"I can find Case for you, if you like, but he's not in his office. This time of the evening he's just finished his round of the kitchens and he's headed back out here to do a bit of mingling. Good for business, you know," he confided.

"I can imagine," Kendra returned smoothly, her eyes going back automatically to the gambling floor. It was early yet, but already the crowd was beginning to thicken rapidly. As she stood beside her official greeter a laughing group of expensively dressed men and women came in out of the snowy night, received an aloof, welcoming nod from the man at her side, and made their way eagerly down the marble steps.

"If you'll wait here, I'll see if I can scare him up," the bouncer volunteered helpfully.

"Thank you . . ." She broke off inquiringly, realizing she didn't know the name of the man with the somewhat beaten-up face.

"Wolf, ma'am," he supplied quickly. "Short for Wolfgang. Wolfgang Amadeus Higgins." He smiled apologetically.

"I see," Kendra responded a little blankly. "Well, then, thank you, uh, Wolf. I would like to get this business with Mr. Garrett out of the way as soon as possible so I can be on my way."

"Sure. If you'll give me your name, I'll tell him you're here."

"My name is Kendra Loring. He won't recognize it," she added with a smile. "You may tell him I'm here over a matter concerning a Mrs. Donna Radburn."

A flash of recognition at the second name lit Wolf's features for an instant and then was diplomatically buried. "Wait here, Miss Loring. I'll find Case."

Kendra stood beside the alabaster railing that circled the gambling area and watched Wolf disappear into the crowd. For a long moment she watched the action below her and wondered idly how Donna had ever been so foolish as to get herself mixed up in the dangerous world of high stakes and high-risk luck. How could all the people in the casino fail to realize the inherent darkness that lay below the glittering surface?

But perhaps that's what attracted them, she decided philosophically, her fingers resting lightly on the rail. The luxurious casino fairly screamed power and money and danger. For some, that would be an irresistible lure. She wondered at the sort of man Case Garrett must be, knowing in her bones he would probably be exactly like his

12

casino. There would be an outer polish bought with money from a source that was probably best left unquestioned, and it would cover the dangerous inner core of the man. Kendra was sure of it.

It seemed clear to her that only a man who had lived a lifetime in the shadowy world of menace and corruption could run such a successful casino. He was probably an ex-gangster and possibly not so "ex," she told herself scornfully. Kendra knew the gambling houses were well policed by the state, but everyone knew the mystique of the dark side of the business clung.

Which was not to say that the gambling was run dishonestly. There was no need, she thought wryly. The odds always favored the house over an individual player.

No, she told herself, she didn't want to hang around here any longer than necessary. Her hazel eyes moved restlessly around the room, momentarily catching sight of her own reflection in the mirror-paneled wall to her left.

She recognized the woman who stared back at her. She ought to have. Kendra spent money and exercised great willpower creating that person. The overall effect was one of remote aloofness, which suited her perfectly.

Unfortunately, because one seldom smiles spontaneously at oneself, she had no idea how that remoteness vanished under the exploding sun of her own smile. Wolf Higgins had seen it, of course. It was the reason he'd jumped so quickly to track down his boss. A lot of people did things for Kendra under the influence of that dazzling smile, which made her hazel eyes glitter beguilingly. Kendra liked to think, however, that people were really responding to the politely masked forcefulness of her not inconsiderable will.

It never occurred to her that people reacted to the smile, because Kendra had never thought of herself as a beauty. There was a strength about her clear, intelligent eyes, straight, no-nonsense nose, and firmly sculpted cheek-bones and chin. Strength, but not beauty.

If pressed and if she happened to be feeling in a self-generous mood, she would have described her assortment of features as reasonably but not overly attractive. But such an average assessment would have failed to denote the hint of sensual fullness in her lower lip, the inner vitality, which expressed itself in a slender, strong body, and the hint of challenge that was reflected in her eyes. She would also have said she looked her age—twenty-nine.

"Attractive" would also have been inadequate to describe the multishaded light-brown hair with its natural hints of sunlight, honey, and warmth. It was worn this night in its usual sleek coil at the back of her head, but on the rare occasions when it was released, the soft brown mass fell to her waist.

The white mink coat seemed to emphasize rather than conceal Kendra's narrow waist, small, high breasts, and full hips. Gold high-heeled sandals accentuated the shapely curves of her legs, made strong by San Francisco hills. Her body was a good one, Kendra liked to think, not because it was voluptuous but because she had made it strong.

Strong and skilled. Never again would she have to fear a man's sexual violence. Never again would she find herself helpless against a man bent on rape.

Deliberately she turned away from that last thought and from the image in the mirror. Her gaze swung back to the gaming floor, searching for Wolf Higgins.

She saw him almost at once, speaking earnestly to a man who had just emerged from an entrance on the far side of the circular gambling arena. Case Garrett, no doubt, Kendra thought, her hazel eyes narrowing in barely concealed dislike.

Her glance went from Wolf's battered face to the face

14

of his boss, and at that precise moment Garrett glanced up and saw her.

The shock was wholly unexpected and unbelievably staggering. Instinctively Kendra found herself grasping the cold railing for support as she met the full force of his one-eyed, night-dark gaze.

She did not know the man, her mind almost shouted, curiously incensed by the strange flash of elemental recognition that arced between herself and Garrett. They had never met! What, then, caused this frightening sense of déjà vu, which threatened to overwhelm her. The temporary vertigo was so strong that for a timeless instant she almost convinced herself that Case Garrett had experienced the same unnerving sensation.

But that was ridiculous. Pure fantasy. Deliberately Kendra willed herself to control the strange tension that gripped her. The fleeting moment passed, mercifully, and reality returned with a rush.

He was, after all, only another man, probably a crook. How could he have affected her so?

She knew he was watching her intently as he listened to Wolf. She felt the power in the dark-eyed gaze, a power which seemed intensified by the black velvet patch he wore on his left eye. It was as if the force of his will was channeled into the remaining orb and somehow doubled.

His gaze never released hers as he stepped down onto the red-carpeted gambling pit and started across the room toward her. Kendra had a sudden desire to turn and flee, but she fought it with self-derision, forcing herself to study the advancing man with cool hauteur.

The power in the compelling darkness of his gaze radiated throughout Case Garrett. Kendra had ample time to register and analyze the magnitude of it as he made his way toward her, Wolf trailing in his wake.

It was there in Garrett's long, gliding stride, which bespoke a smoothly coordinated body. It was in the arrogant set of his broad shoulders and the supple leanness of his tapered waist and hips. And it was uncompromisingly mirrored in his face, which had seen far too much in its time.

Automatically Kendra estimated his age at around thirty-six or thirty-seven. And, as with Wolf, she was willing to hazard a guess that his apprenticeship had been in a tough school. It showed glaringly, to her eyes at least, through the expensive white silk of his shirt and the fine black broadcloth evening jacket and close-fitting trousers.

His hair was black; as black as the sixteen-hundred-foot depths of Lake Tahoe. But there was a hint of moonlight in it, Kendra thought fancifully. A faint rippling of silver showed at his temples. The black pelt was neatly combed back and away from the wide, intelligent forehead, and at the back, it almost touched the crisp white of his collar.

There was a silky, sooty fringe of lashes around his dark eye, the softness of which did nothing to relieve the harsh contours of his face. The power and male arrogance of Garrett was clearly detailed in the high thrust of his cheekbones, the aggressive strength of his nose, and the implacable line of his jaw and chin. Not a handsome man—a hard man.

He was dark and dangerous, Kendra concluded. A man one could easily come to fear, her feminine heart added. Yet, she knew beyond a doubt that it was that femaleness in her that had reacted so violently to the initial shock of seeing him. Her fingers tightened on the railing, and she lifted her head in unconscious defiance. No, she did not know this man.

Only business had brought her to the fringes of his environment tonight, and she would take great care to stay on her side of the border, she decided as he covered the last of the distance between them. She watched him take the marble steps with an easy, catlike grace, and then he was in front of her.

He wasn't as tall as the massive Wolf, she reflected abstractedly, less than six feet, but he nevertheless seemed to dwarf her own five and a half feet.

As if in protective retaliation against the unwarranted sense of recognition she had experienced on first seeing him, Kendra made no attempt to hide her condemnation of the man and all he represented. Her eyes dropped deliberately over the fine clothing, letting him know subtly that she saw the shark underneath the surface.

She knew he had absorbed and understood the impact of her censorious glance. Something ominous flickered in the depths of his dark gaze, and then he spoke.

"Miss Loring? I'm Case Garrett. I'm told you wish to speak to me."

The voice fit the man, deep and dark and outwardly polite. A voice that could seduce a woman or tear her to pieces. At the moment it hovered in neutral territory, as if waiting to see which tactic would be necessary with her.

"My business concerns Donna Radburn," she told him in her own cool, slightly husky tones.

"So Wolf said. Would you care to come to my office?"

Without a word she turned and walked beside him, aware of Wolf's eyes on them as the pair moved around the promenade that circled the gambling floor.

"I gather you managed to thoroughly disconcert poor Wolf by speaking genuine French to him at the door," Case remarked, slanting a speculative glance down at Kendra's deliberately impassive features as he led her along a plushly carpeted hall. "That wasn't very kind. He's worked hard on that accent."

"I'm sorry, Mr. Garrett," she responded coolly, stepping past him as he indicated an open door. "But I wasn't in the mood to go along with the fantasy. I'm here on business."

"Pity," he murmured dryly, shutting the door behind

him, "considering how much money has been spent on the fantasy. May I take your coat?"

She unbelted the expensive fur, submitting to his small act of gallantry in removing it from her shoulders. Kendra knew his eye moved with interest over the slender sheath of blood-red silk she wore, but she ignored the masculine glance, her own gaze taking in the elegantly restrained decor of his office.

Thick gray patterned carpet flowed from wall to wall, the color repeated in the velvet-covered chairs. A heavy black glass desk dominated the room, and there was a designer's touch in the accents of white and tan elsewhere.

Her dress made a splash of silky flame across the gray velvet chair as she took a seat. Without hesitation she unzipped the hidden pocket of the white muff and withdrew a check.

"I've brought this on Donna's behalf. It's not the full amount she tells me she owes, but it's nearly half. The rest will be available in a couple of months."

Case Garrett sank into the black leather seat behind the desk and reached for the check, scanning it quickly before glancing up to find Kendra's cool, faintly accusing eyes on him. The dark gaze narrowed and hardened as he took in her expression. Briefly Kendra found herself wondering how he'd lost his left eye. Then she put the question aside. It was no business of hers.

"I get the impression this whole task has been somewhat distasteful for you, Miss Loring," he observed calmly, a hint of deliberate baiting nearly buried in the soft words.

"Very. Now, if I may have some sort of receipt for the amount of that check, I will be on my way."

"Why did Donna send you? Why didn't she come herself?" Case asked, idly leaning back in the chair and making no obvious move to write out a receipt.

"There are reasons, Mr. Garrett. The receipt, please?"

He glanced again at the check. "The amount Mrs. Radburn owes is considerably in excess of this," he drawled slowly.

"I'm aware of that. As I said, you'll have the rest in a couple of months."

"The total was due last month," he told her flatly.

"What are you going to do? Send Wolf out to beat her up?" Kendra inquired evenly, her dislike of the situation plain in her voice.

"On the contrary, Miss Loring. There are other ways for a woman to pay her gambling debts. Don't look so shocked. That's exactly the sort of remark you were expecting me to make, wasn't it? I can see your opinion of my . . . er . . . profession quite clearly in those lovely hazel eyes!"

"From what little I know of your line of work, Mr. Garrett," Kendra retorted acidly, "I doubt that you would allow one of your customers to pay off her debts in anything other than cold, hard cash."

"There are exceptions to every rule," he mused, his dark eye glinting with mockery. "Do you gamble, Miss Loring?"

"I have other uses for my money, Mr. Garrett."

"Your own, perhaps, but would you have any serious objections to throwing away a man's money on my tables?"

"This conversation is becoming a bit personal," Kendra said quietly. "May I please have the receipt for that check?"

"You'll have to give me a moment to consider this," he drawled. "The debt is, after all, somewhat overdue, and you have only brought half of the required amount."

"Are you going to refuse Donna's check?" she demanded coolly, wondering at the small shiver of apprehension that had just coursed down the length of her spine. This was an unforseen contingency. Donna had felt certain there would be no problem. . . .

"No," he said after a second's hesitation. "I shall be willing to accept the partial payment, under certain conditions."

"What conditions?" Kendra asked, meeting his challenging look with determined unconcern. She refused to give way to the irrational impulse to twist her hands together in her lap. Instead she concentrated her inner energy on sitting serenely in the gray chair as if she were content to humor him for the moment.

"You needn't be so wary, Miss Loring," he soothed, a lazy smile revealing the whiteness of shark's teeth. "I'm merely asking you to join me for dinner."

She flinched at the unexpected demand, regrouping her forces at once. "Asking me or telling me you won't accept that check unless I do?" she tossed back bluntly, anger beginning to simmer under the surface of her calm.

"That's putting it a little crudely—"

"A simple yes or no will do," she interrupted icily, telling herself that if she remained resolute enough, there was still a chance she could face him down. He was playing with her. He had every intention of accepting that check; she was certain of it. But what if he did refuse? The last thing Donna needed now was another dangerous male making threats!

"Are you always so straightforward, Miss Loring?" Case inquired interestedly.

"When I'm conducting business, yes."

He winced. "You consider a dinner invitation business?"

"In this instance, it would be more akin to blackmail."

"Another line of work in which you would expect to find me adept?"

"I'd rather not discuss your methods of making a living, Mr. Garrett."

"I can see that," he murmured, sitting forward and twisting a key in the desk drawer.

Kendra watched worriedly as he dropped Donna's check inside but made no move to write out any sort of receipt.

"Mr. Garrett," she began firmly, fighting for control in her words.

"Call me Case," he admonished, getting easily to his feet. "All my friends do!" He grinned at her, a purely male, purely bantering smile, which dared her to tell him they weren't friends.

"The response to that is obvious," she gritted.

Out of a vague feeling of self-defense, she also rose to her feet, the white mink muff dangling on a silken cord from one wrist. She saw him glance at the refined elegance of gold at her throat and ears, and then his smile broadened knowingly.

"Oh, you'll like being my friend," he told her softly, coming close but not touching her. "I'm very generous to my friends. And you look like a woman who appreciates a man's generosity."

The open insult was almost more than even Kendra's hard-won willpower could tolerate. Red washed up into her cheeks and then receded, leaving her pale in the chandelier's light. She wanted to scream at him that every expensive item of her clothing had been purchased by her, not a man, but instinct warned that he would only take pleasure in having provoked a response.

"The casino restaurant has an excellent chef, Kendra," Case went on urbanely, using her first name quite naturally. "I'm sure you'll enjoy the roast duckling, and the house pâté is exceptional."

"Why are you doing this, Mr. Garrett?" Kendra whispered with barely repressed anger.

He took her arm and led her toward the door. "Mostly,

I think, because you so clearly dislike me and my business," he told her with blatant honesty.

Kendra hesitated, thinking of the check in his drawer. She needed that receipt for Donna's peace of mind. For Donna's sake, she could tolerate dinner with this one-eyed shark. Belatedly, she told herself she shouldn't have challenged him so openly.

"You enjoy dining with women who dislike you." She sighed in the tone of one resigning oneself to a particularly unpleasant business chore.

"I enjoy dining with women who interest me," he corrected, opening the door with grave politeness. "And you, Miss Kendra Loring, interest me. Greatly."

"I can only regret that," she told him ruefully.

"I can see that. Perhaps the penalty you're paying for your poor manners will serve to teach you better ones," he noted suavely.

She ignored that. "You'll give me the receipt after dinner?"

"Yes," he agreed pleasantly enough, guiding her down the hall in the opposite direction of the gambling area.

"I have your word on that?" she clarified cautiously.

"You do, although I can't imagine you'd put much faith in it."

Kendra bit her lip, refraining from the sort of sharp response that would only serve to goad him further. She had made a mistake in handling this man, she acknowledged privately. She should have been polite and charming, and she should have smiled. She should have been all those things, yet instead she had been cold, condemning, and, yes, arrogant. Not a good way to conduct business.

She gave a mental, philosophical shrug. Well, she doubted that she was in any real danger with him, and if he were to try something physical, she could deal with it. But somehow Kendra didn't think it would come to that. He was just out to get her back for her haughty manner.

Not an unpredictable reaction if she'd just given the subject some thought earlier.

She would tolerate dinner and chalk up the event to experience. The next time she dealt with a man whose background probably could not bear close scrutiny, she would take care not to insult him too obviously! She took a long breath. Perhaps the meal would pass more serenely if she mended a few fences first.

"Mr. Garrett . . ."

"Call me Case, or I'll insist you stick around for dessert." He smiled deliberately.

"Case," she repeated dutifully, summoning an apologetic curve of her lips that was not repeated in her eyes. "I'm sorry I offended you, but this whole thing has been rather a nuisance for me. I'm doing a favor for Donna, and—"

"I only accept the most sincerely meant apologies," he told her coolly, coming to a halt by an elevator and pressing the button. "So let's skip that line about feeling bad for having offended me. Quite unnecessary anyway. I've endured much worse," he added cryptically.

For some reason the mildness of the statement struck Kendra as so incongruous as to be very funny. A smile sailed into her eyes, and the curve of her mouth took on the spontaneous brilliance that had so overcome Wolf a short time earlier.

"I'll just bet you have." She laughed up at him, imagining the sort of "offenses" a man like this must have been dealt in his life. "Did you punish the offenders by taking them out to dinner? Strange, but I wouldn't have thought you the 'turn the other cheek' type."

"You don't think having dinner with me will be such a trying penalty?" he murmured, his dark eye drinking in the sight of her smile with a strangely thirsty look that Kendra didn't understand.

"Not if the duckling is as good as you say it is," she

23

retorted blandly. "Besides, I'm hungry," she added easily, stepping obediently into the opening doors of the wood-paneled elevator. "I was going to have dinner after I finished my business here, anyway." She watched him press the button for the third floor of the building. "Is the restaurant on the top floor?"

"No," he replied, flicking an amused glance at her inquiring expression. "My apartments are."

"Your apartments!" she snapped, the well-marked lines of her brows snapping together in a quelling frown. "You invited me to dinner in the restaurant. . . ."

The elevator was already gliding to a halt, the heavy doors opening to reveal a white-carpeted hallway and a broad, carved oak door directly across from them.

"I invited you to dinner. I don't recall saying we would dine in the restaurant," he said smoothly, guiding her across the hall and inserting a key into the massively ornate brass lock.

He opened the door but made no move to force her inside. Instead he smiled with deliberate, goading mockery as she hesitated on the threshold.

"The deal still stands," he told her easily. "Roast duckling in exchange for Mrs. Radburn's receipt. How good a friend of hers are you, Kendra?"

"Good enough to eat your duckling," she replied crisply, her eyes narrowed in warning. "But not good enough to play the role of dessert. Is that very clear, Case?"

"Very," he admitted dryly. "The invitation was for dinner, not bed."

"As long as that's understood," Kendra began magnanimously and walked into the room. She could take care of herself, but that didn't mean she wanted to find it necessary to do so, she thought grimly.

"Willing to humor me up to a point, hmmm?" he observed, shutting the door and standing with his back to it as he watched her take in the room.

"I suppose so," she acknowledged, and then she stopped short at the sight of the apartment spread out before her. "Good heavens, Case! Since when do professional gamblers create fantasy worlds for themselves?"

"Everyone needs an escape."

"But a South Sea island?" Kendra asked skeptically, eyeing the wooden ceiling fan, the tapa-cloth-covered rattan furniture, the woven grass mat on which she stood, and the bamboo trellis that separated the entrance hall from the sunken living room. Potted palms, a painting of a sailing ship, and some unusual baskets accessorized a room which would have been appropriate for a tropical island.

It was an expensively done fantasy, she acknowledged privately, but a startling contrast to the snows of winter in Lake Tahoe. Somehow, when she pivoted on one heel to face her host, it struck Kendra that Case Garrett looked right at home in his exotic surroundings. He was unique enough to fit the fantasy of the room. A born adventurer.

"Can you think of a better setting in which to warm some answers from a very cool and aloof mystery woman?" He smiled meaningfully.

"I'm not here to give you answers tonight, Case," she said quietly and with absolute confidence. "I'm only here to buy that receipt."

"That would be a shame," he told her, his gaze darkening. "Because you have some answers to questions I didn't even know I wanted to ask until I saw you waiting for me across the casino tonight."

Kendra saw the deliberate challenge in him, and her expressive mouth quirked wryly. It had been two long years since she had last come in contact with a man who viewed women as potential prey.

She wasn't yet certain whether or not Case Garrett represented a genuine threat, but one thing she *was* sure of: The past two years had not been wasted. Kendra Loring would never again be forced into the role of unwilling victim by any man. She had learned to take care of herself, and she possessed the inner confidence that that knowledge provided.

No, she felt sublimely assured of her personal safety. Case Garrett wouldn't want a major scene in his own casino, anyway. That wasn't really what bothered her, she realized as she stepped down into the fantasy room.

Her main concern was that she had finally put a name to that strange flash of recognition she had experienced earlier in the casino. The other word for it was "attraction."

CHAPTER TWO

It was as if the illusion of the room somehow reached out to surround her, Kendra decided later. The very incongruousness of the decor gave her a curious sense of unreality, as though she had stepped into an isolated moment out of time with a man she would normally have had nothing to do with.

This couldn't be her, she told herself in silent humor, dining in South Seas elegance on roast duckling in orange sauce and drinking fine wine. And this certainly couldn't be her engaging in tantalizing, delicate conversation with a man she should despise.

But here in this tropical setting, which looked out on moonlit snow-covered mountains, darkened forests and lake, nothing was quite as it should be.

But it didn't really matter, Kendra thought deliberately as she swirled the wine in her long-stemmed glass. After all, she would never see this dark, mysterious man again. The whole evening was a bizarre vignette in an otherwise graciously calm, sophisticated life.

Case set his gleaming silver knife and fork correctly on the English china plate, pushed both gently aside, and leaned forward to rest his chin on linked fingers. The black velvet patch lent him an undeniably buccaneerish air, especially in this island scene.

"We're very good at this, aren't we?" he mused, his gaze gleaming with a combination of humor and frustration.

"Very good at what?" Kendra smiled, her glance flickering away for an instant to the new-falling snow outside the window. The soft, wintry sight might as well have been a movie she was viewing for all the reality it had from the perspective of her rattan chair.

"Carrying on a conversation without managing to drop a single, concrete fact about ourselves. I've been plying you with good food and wine for over an hour, and I can still count all the pieces of hard information I've learned about you on the fingers of one hand."

"As you said, it's a mutual talent," she murmured, thinking that every time she had come close to a serious inquiry about his past or his life outside the casino, he had turned the question aside with an enigmatic smile and a light comment. Perhaps he didn't want the potentially grim answers casting a shadow over the fantasy, she thought.

"You're very confident," he continued gently. "Very self-assured. And you're driving me crazy trying to pry information out of you!"

She laughed at that, pleased at his admission of powerlessness. "Why do you need the mundane facts of my life? Are you making a scrapbook?"

"Hardly worth it so far," he retorted dryly. He held up one hand and began enumerating. "At this point I know your name"—he broke off to lift a black brow inquiringly—"assuming, of course, that you gave Wolf the real one. Did you?"

"I don't see that it matters particularly."

He sighed. "So even that fact is in doubt. What else? I know you're on a mission for one of my former patrons. Does Donna still live in Los Angeles, by the way?" he added innocently.

"As far as I know," Kendra said smoothly.

"Can I assume you're also from L.A., then?"

"You can if you like."

28

His mouth curved wryly as he held up a third finger. "I know you enjoy good food and expensive clothes. . . ."

She shrugged. There wasn't much to be said about that. She had demolished her duckling with delicate greed. And the mink and silk spoke for themselves.

"You see?" He groaned. "Very few hard facts."

"I know little more than that about you," she pointed out, lounging back against the tapa-cloth print of the cushions on her chair and smiling at him across the gleaming table. The lovely meal and table setting had emerged miraculously after a short phone call. Once the food had been delivered, no one had returned to intrude. Kendra wondered how frequently Case Garrett entertained in this fashion.

"Tell me what you've learned," he invited with a coolly mocking twist of his mouth.

"Your name, assuming it's the right one, of course," she drawled obediently.

"It's on the casino license. Which is more proof than you've provided me," he told her virtuously.

She inclined her head briefly, acknowledging the point. "I know you're the employer of one Wolfgang Amadeus Higgins. . . . Where did you find him, incidentally?" she asked interestedly.

"Wolf and I go back a long way," Case retorted, telling her nothing at all.

"I know you run one of the most exclusive clubs in Nevada . . ."

"A profession of which you obviously do not wholly approve."

"It's your business," she said amicably.

"Literally," he agreed.

She glanced at the fingers of her left hand and gave up. "We're about even, I think. Although I suppose I could add that your taste in interior decor is not quite what I would have expected."

He glanced around the lush room and smiled slowly. "If I tell you why the apartment is decorated this way, will you answer a personal question in return?"

She hesitated, eyeing him with consideration that was spiked with laughter. She really did want to know why he had chosen this particular fantasy. "If the question is not too personal, yes," she said.

He rose, coming around the small table to assist her to her feet, and lead her over to the couch. Gallantly he seated her in one corner and went to a side table of glass and wicker to pour a brandy for each of them. Carrying them back to the couch, he handed her one of the snifters and sat down next to her, not touching.

"I worked in that part of the world once," he began rather cautiously, staring down into the golden brandy as he warmed it with his hands. "I love it."

She waited. "End of explanation?" she finally prompted, watching his hard profile. His blind eye was on the side away from her.

"Sometimes explanations are very simple," he said, sitting back into the depths of the couch in a lazy, graceful sprawl. He turned to look at her. "I'll be satisfied with an equally simple answer from you."

"I have to hear the question first."

He smiled beguilingly, making her supremely conscious of the unaccountable attraction he seemed to hold for her. She was suddenly aware of an answering shiver of response. It made no sense, but it nevertheless caused the glass in her hand to quiver ever so slightly.

"Will you let me kiss you tonight before you leave?"

Kendra blinked and then lowered her lashes, not out of false modesty but rather out of confusion. She told herself she hadn't been expecting this, and in a way she was right. A part of her hadn't expected him to *ask* for the kiss. She

30

had anticipated that he would take it. But he was deliberately making her accept responsibility for the action, and that was confusing.

"I don't think that would be very wise," she said quietly, taking a sip of the brandy and letting its fire counteract the faint trembling. My God! What was she doing here, dining with a man who ran a casino? A man who employed people like Wolf Higgins. It was time she got out of this strange fantasy, Kendra thought resolutely, setting down her glass.

"May I have the receipt now?" she inquired politely, getting to her feet.

"You didn't answer my question," he reminded her, gliding up lazily to stand beside her.

She shook her head bemusedly. "This has been a most unusual evening," she began politely.

"Meaning you don't normally have dinner with men who have a bit of an unsavory element about them." He chuckled. "But it's not your fault, remember. I blackmailed you into it, as I recall."

"So you did." She nodded purposefully. "And now that I've paid the ransom, don't you think it's time you concluded your end of the deal?"

"If you're not going to give me a direct no in response to my simple question, it can only mean one thing," he whispered in a voice that deepened to a husky, sexy drawl. Deliberately he put out his hand and gently cupped her chin. "It can only mean yes."

Kendra didn't move, curiously mesmerized by the sensual electricity that was flowing around her. She felt almost trapped in the illusory cocoon he had spun around them both tonight, unable to turn her head aside as he lowered his to take her lips.

If he had forced the kiss, her response would have been unequivocal. She would have refused it with equal force, and the violence would have shattered the spell in the room. But he was far too wise for such an action, she realized as his mouth covered hers.

The kiss was slow, warm, questing, and it began subtly, almost experimentally. At first Case made no move to draw her more securely into his arms, content, it seemed, to taste her essence and let her experience his.

Kendra was vividly aware of his body heat as he stood so close, touching her only with one hand. She had an almost instinctive desire to lessen the small space between them. His fingers moved delicately, sensitively along her throat, shaping the curve of her jaw and sliding down warmly to the collar of the red silk dress.

His lips moved sensuously over hers, coaxing, persuading, exploring. At her sides, her nails suddenly turned inward against her palms, and she felt a faint, stifled moan at the back of her throat.

As if that were a signal for which he had been waiting, Case reached out with his other hand, curving it around her waist and pulling her slowly against him.

"You have the most delightful scent," he rasped against her lips. "Clean, fresh, warm, sweet . . . like an island breeze. . . ."

She lifted her hands automatically, spreading her fingertips across the hardness of his shoulders. She felt the masculine solidity of his body, and luxuriated in it unthinkingly. She was almost thirty years old, and she had been kissed often enough during those years, but never quite like this, her mind whispered seductively, never with quite this tender, probing persuasiveness.

Somewhere a faint warning bell was ringing, but for the moment Kendra told herself she could safely ignore it. Soon she would leave and never see this man or his casino again. Knowing that she would be safe enough shortly was a kind of incentive to enjoy this stolen hour with a man she would normally have never allowed into her world.

But he hadn't broached her environment, she thought

32

vaguely. It was she who had invaded his tonight. And the temptation to let the kiss linger for a little longer was overwhelming.

"Kendra . . . ?"

Her name was uttered in a deep, hoarse voice as his hand tightened around her slender waist. She heard the soft rustle of her red silk dress as his fingers found the shape of her.

"Kendra, you intrigue me. Do you realize that?" he asked in a muffled groan.

"I think I'd better be going," she managed hesitantly, knowing she should withdraw herself from this strange world.

But he ignored the words, taking advantage of her parted lips to abruptly deepen the kiss. She felt the seductive assault of his tongue, and she trembled slightly. She knew the small movement communicated itself to him, because of the way he shifted his hold to mold her more completely against him.

Without thinking about it Kendra lifted her hands to the darkness of his hair, her fingertips finding the band of the velvet patch before exploring further to bury themselves at the back of his neck.

"Ah," she breathed as the dangerous, warm languor stole over her, arousing something faint and exciting deep within her body.

His hands slid down to the small of her back, pressing, urging, and kneading with growing arousal.

"At least you're not going to remain a total mystery tonight," he growled as he reluctantly pulled back from her mouth and began a trail of tiny, glowing kisses along the line of her cheek, just below her eye. "But don't you realize that every question you answer only raises a thousand more?"

"They're questions that don't need answering," she

whispered, turning her lips against the sun-browned length of his throat.

"I disagree, but we can argue about it later."

His hands cupped her hips, arching her against his lower body, making her aware of the rising passion in him. It stirred a response in her, heightened the light-headed recklessness that was beginning to take hold. The warning bell still sounded, and still she ignored it.

"I want you," he said with heavy bluntness, his male desire plain. "You must know that by now. Will you stay with me tonight, mystery woman?"

In spite of herself Kendra sucked in her breath at the straightforward, uncompromising question.

"No," she finally said softly, closing her eyes against the feel of his lips on the nape of her neck. "That's impossible."

"Nothing is impossible."

"What you ask is," she returned flatly, but making no move to pull away from his warmth and hardness. He was using his tongue and then his teeth on the ultrasensitive skin at the back of her neck as she pressed her face into his shoulder. The sensation was an exquisite little torment that made her cling to him with tiny claws.

"Do you know that I wanted to ask you to spend the night the moment I looked up and saw you across the casino?" he murmured. "There was something between us from the first instant of eye contact. Do you deny it?"

"There was only a matter of business between us," she protested softly.

"No. There is more . . . much more. Aren't you curious to stay and find out?"

"I won't be staying, Case. That's very, very final."

"I can tell from the tone of your voice," he agreed broodingly. He curled his fingers into the softness of her. "Will you ever be back?"

"No."

"Not even to pay off the last half of Donna's debt?"

"By then she'll be able to do it herself."

"I see. You really don't approve of me, do you?"

"My approval hardly matters, Case."

"So I keep telling myself," he retorted dryly.

He shifted his weight, pulling her down onto the couch beside him and gathering her back into his arms. For a long moment there were no more words, but his hands began to rove over her, caressing the shape of one thigh, the silk of her dress rustling gently.

Kendra didn't try to restrict his hand until she felt his palm flatten on her stomach and glide upward to a point just beneath her breasts. Then, at last, she began to listen to the warnings in her mind.

Unwillingly she began to ease away, a rueful smile shaping her mouth as her lashes fluttered open. She met his heated gaze and started to say something witty and conclusive. But before the clever words could form into a sentence, he put his hand on her breast.

"Case!"

His name was a reflexive little cry compounded of protest and the need he had stirred in her. She knew she was trembling again, and when his fingers sought the nipple through the silk, she wanted to slap his hand aside. But somehow she couldn't do it. Not yet. And he saw the ambivalence in her eyes.

"You can't deny your own response, my little mystery woman," he said in deep satisfaction as the tip of her breast hardened beneath his touch.

"Please don't touch me like that," Kendra said huskily.

"Will you touch me?" he countered whimsically, taking his hand away from her soft curves and lifting her fingertips to the side of his cheek. When she touched him, he turned his mouth against the skin of her palm and kissed her with a passion that seemed all the more intense for being so well leashed.

35

Kendra breathed in the musky, intoxicating scent of his vibrant maleness and took a firm grip on her senses. Her fantasy night had gone far enough. It was time to escape to reality.

"I want to leave now, Case," she said very quietly, very resolutely. "May I please have Donna's receipt?"

He dropped another lingering caress against her wrist, and then slowly lowered her hand. "You're really going?"

"Yes."

He stared at her for another long second, and she could feel the will in him growing. He was deliberately exerting it, she realized, trying to make her change her mind. But that, as she had told him, was impossible. Half smiling, she shook her head in silent response.

The bizarre interlude had held a temptation she would never have expected to encounter, but it was time to end it. She had no intention of getting involved with this strange, enigmatic man whose world was so far removed from her own.

"The receipt?" she prompted gently, certain that she would get it. It may not have been a totally rational certainty, given who and what he undoubtedly was. But after the evening they had just shared, Kendra felt confident she could trust him that much. He'd told her he would let her have it. She'd believed him.

"Nothing I can say or do will make you reconsider?" he asked slowly.

Again she shook her head, the faint smile still quirking her lips.

"The receipt is my only hold on you," he pointed out, stroking the veins of her small wrist with a circling thumb. The small, erotic touch was sending sparks throughout her body.

"But you won't use it," Kendra stated positively. "You gave me your word I could have it after dinner."

"Did you enjoy dinner?" he asked with a wry expression.

"Very much," she said honestly.

"Very gracious of you," he applauded, "given that I rather coerced you into it." He stood up, tossed a last, speculative glance down at her, and then walked across the room. "I'll get your receipt."

She watched him disappear down a hallway, and then concentrated her attention on the still-falling snow outside the huge window. What an evening this had evolved into, she thought. Somehow she didn't think she would ever forget it. And she had the good sense not to try and repeat it!

"This will ease Donna's mind," Case said a few minutes later as he came back into the living room, a note with his signature on it in his hand. He held it out, and Kendra took it, folding it and stuffing it into the white muff.

"My coat?" she said politely. It had been left in his office.

"We can get it on the way out," he told her, opening a bamboo-trimmed closet and reaching for an overcoat.

"There's no need to see me back to the hotel," she said quickly, forestalling him as she awakened to his intention.

"Of course there is," he disagreed coolly.

"Case, I don't want you taking me back."

He must have heard the steel in her words, because he stopped in the process of shrugging into the coat and stared at her. Once again there was a short but intense battle of wills, and once again Case backed down.

"You want everything to end right here, don't you?" he said with sudden understanding. His gaze hardened.

"It's the only way."

"Why?" he asked starkly.

"Case, I've already spent far more time with you than I had ever intended. I want to conclude our business and leave. Alone."

He surveyed her rigid, determined stance, and then turned to replace the wool coat in the closet. "You will allow me to at least see you to the front door of the casino?" he drawled.

It occurred to her that she had annoyed him, and Kendra relaxed, moving toward the door. "If you insist," she murmured.

"The soul of gracious femininity," he muttered, opening the door for her.

"Are you going to turn surly at this stage?" she inquired humorously, quite confident now.

For an instant there was a look of warning in the darkness of his eye, and an almost infinitesimal flicker of fear coursed along her spine. It was over almost before it had begun, but not before it had served to remind Kendra that everything she knew about this man indicated a potential for danger. She could take care of herself, but it was foolish to play too long with fire. It was stupid to go looking for unnecessary trouble, even if it would be satisfying to prove to herself that she could handle it now.

And then he was smiling; a cold, polite smile that barely changed the shape of his hard mouth. "I shall try to behave as far as the front entrance," he told her.

The ride down in the elevator to the first level was accomplished in silence. In silence, too, her coat was retrieved, and in silence she was walked to the front door.

Wolf Higgins glanced interestedly but politely at his boss and then at Kendra.

"Do you want me to get the car, Case?"

"No," Kendra interrupted. "I'll take one of the cabs out front."

Wolf smiled at her but waited for Case's instructions.

"I'm afraid she means it," Case informed the other man with a wry smile. "A very determined woman, our Miss Loring." He swung around to face Kendra. "Good night, Kendra."

She thought he was going to kiss her, and to make certain that it didn't happen, Kendra stepped away.

"Good night, Case . . . Wolf."

Without a word Wolf stepped through the decorated glass door and hailed a waiting cab. She thanked him with a smile and, getting inside, settled back for the short drive. The smile lingered on her mouth as she gazed out at the cold, snowy night. After the warmth of Case's tropical island it was a shock to come back out into it. But she understood his fantasy retreat, she realized suddenly, surprised to find she had anything at all in common with such a man. She understood his home, because she had deliberately constructed such a gracious retreat for herself. True, her choice of home surroundings had taken a slightly different twist—Kendra's smile widened as she remembered her gracious French decor—but the principle was the same in some ways. It was as if they both had created the world they wanted around them in so far as it was possible. Life, Kendra thought, repeating her personal philosophy, was what you made it. A person had to decide what he or she wanted and then make it happen. Instinctively she felt Case would understand that philosophy.

She got out of the cab at the wrong hotel, intending to walk to hers. It would be simple for Wolf to question the cab driver when he returned to the club. There were several people out on the streets, moving cheerfully from one brightly lit casino to the next, in search of better luck. Kendra felt the ebb and flow around her but paid little attention as she walked briskly.

She hadn't wanted Case to escort her back tonight for several reasons, not the least of which was that it seemed safest not to allow him to find out anything more about her than he already had.

She could take some pride in having fended off his gently persistent questioning during dinner. He had hidden his frustration well, but she'd sensed it.

Had that been why he had kissed her? To make her more amenable to questioning? But why should he really care about her background? She supposed she had been a minor curiosity in his world. An amusing interlude. Would he check out the hotel where she'd gotten out of the cab? Would he be a little upset to find she'd left a false trail?

An amusing interlude, she repeated. That was exactly how she would view the evening. A stopover in a different world. Strange, but the past few hours had been the most interesting she had spent in the past two years!

She was almost at the entrance of her hotel when she caught sight of a dark figure behind her, reflected in the neon-lit glass. Kendra frowned. She had seen that figure earlier, shortly after she'd alighted from the cab.

Her mouth tightened ominously. Had Case followed her, after all? She glanced over her shoulder, half in annoyance. The dark figure disappeared.

Would Case act so craftily? It didn't seem like him somehow. She could imagine him deciding to follow her out of curiosity, but she didn't think he'd duck behind a wall or slip into an open doorway if he thought she'd seen him.

Kendra smiled again. Chances were she would never have seen him in the first place if he'd decided to trail her back to the hotel. He struck her as being much too competent to be that sloppy.

No, she had made a mistake, she decided, standing aside as a surge of people poured out the hotel door. Then she made her way inside, walking straight past the slot machines and diving into the milling crowd surrounding the acres of gambling tables. If someone was following her, she'd lose him here in this chaos.

When she finally made her way to the elevator lobby, there was no one around. Everyone was out participating in the lively nightlife, which had lured people there in the first place. A famous singer was appearing in the lounge, and those who weren't paying a fortune to hear him were spending fortunes at the tables. She had the plush elevator to herself when she finally headed for her room.

She knew she was not alone in the long hall the moment she stepped out of the elevator. Small prickles of alertness were dancing across her shoulders, raising the fine hair at the back of her neck.

What was the matter with her? She was overreacting to the memory of the dark figure she'd spotted on the way back. That must be it. But she'd been taught to heed her body's senses, and so she didn't completely close her mind to the possibility of danger. It was remote but it was there.

And when she crossed the junction of another connecting hall, she knew for certain something was wrong. Very coolly she refrained from the temptation of glancing at the dark male figure who stood supposedly fumbling with a door key.

It wasn't Case, which put a whole new light on the situation. A very dangerous light. Telling herself to be calm, Kendra withdrew her room key from the muff and fitted it to her door lock. Her adrenaline was flowing now, pumping faster and faster through her veins.

She did not allow the sudden increase in energy and alertness to destroy her outward calm. She forced herself to think and act coolly, deliberately, professionally.

She walked into the thickly carpeted room and turned with great casualness to close the door. As she had known there would be, a man appeared suddenly in the opening.

"May I help you?" she asked with mocking politeness, her hand on the door. He was a sleazy looking character, she decided dispassionately, lacking Wolf's interesting flair as well as his scars. This man didn't look as if he'd fought his way to his current station in life. He looked as if he'd arrived via more slimy, less physical means.

He was of an indeterminate age, probably late thirties,

with a knife blade of a nose, a thin frame, and hard blue eyes. He also didn't look overly intelligent. His rather worn suit implied his current job didn't pay well, but then Kendra decided this was the sort of man who could make a new suit of clothes look old and shabby within minutes of putting it on. Some attempt had been made to control his straggling sandy hair with hair oil, but it hadn't been very effective.

"Miss Kendra Loring?" he rasped, stepping over the threshold and reaching for the edge of the door.

"What do you want?" she asked placidly.

"A little information," he told her derisively.

"Sorry, you'll have to get in line. You're not the only one looking for information from me tonight." Kendra firmly pushed the door shut, only to have him retaliate with a strong shove.

"No jokes tonight, lady. I ain't in the mood."

Kendra carefully stepped out of her high-heeled sandals. "If you don't leave me alone, I will call the front desk," she announced icily.

"You'll never make it to the phone," he told her with a slow, anticipatory smile.

"Did Radburn send you?" she inquired with apparent interest, her eyes never leaving his pinched face. This was a man who would telegraph his actions, and he was clearly confident that because he was facing a woman, he was in complete control.

"You and I are going to have a little talk," he hissed, moving with abrupt force into the room and yanking the door shut behind him. "And just to make sure you don't get any clever ideas about screaming . . ."

He started toward her with outstretched hands.

CHAPTER THREE

What happened next took place so quickly, so efficiently, and so automatically, Kendra didn't have time to be astonished at her own ability. She only knew the skill was there when she needed it, just as her instructor had promised.

In the short span of time it took for the weasellike man to reach for her, Kendra's mind switched gears. In a flash she was standing barefooted on the mat back in the San Francisco dojo, dressed in the loose white trousers and jacket called a *judo-gi*. The man coming toward her seemed incredibly off-balance to her trained eye, and she waited for him almost impatiently.

The technique she used would have appeared deceptively easy to an observer, who would have no way of knowing the importance of timing to the success of the throw.

When the attacking man grasped her, Kendra stepped backward about six inches, forcing him to move his weight onto his left foot in order to steady himself. She shifted her weight again, sweeping her opponent's left foot from under him with the sole of her right foot applied just under his ankle.

Simultaneously she pulled down on his left lapel and used a pushing, circular motion with his right sleeve. There was an astounded expression on the narrow, slit-eyed face as the man fell heavily to the green carpet. She had used his own momentum and weight against him with swift sureness, which had turned him from attacker to victim.

As soon as the throw was completed Kendra stepped away, the hotel room snapping back immediately into focus. Something was wrong. The slimy man hadn't fallen the way her opponents at the dojo always fell. There had been a sharp crack, and he had landed in a too-silent sprawl at her feet.

Her momentary exhilaration was squelched almost before it began. Alarmed, she dropped to her knees beside the limp figure. It occurred to her he must have struck his head on the edge of the long, low chest of drawers as he went down.

The blood drained from her face, and her knuckles pressed agitatedly against her mouth as Kendra came alive to the fact that she might have seriously injured or even killed a man.

Horrified at the paleness of the weasellike face, Kendra tried to pull her thoughts together and figure out what to do. Would anyone believe her when she explained the situation? With shaking fingers, she reached out to find the pulse at the base of the man's throat.

She was fumbling for a sign of life in her victim when the hotel-room door swung open, and she glanced up with stunned eyes to see Case Garrett filling the doorway. She was irrationally glad to see him.

"Case! Oh, God! I think I've killed him!"

Without thinking Kendra scrambled to her feet, hurling herself toward the grim-faced man as he stepped silently into the room and shut the door. She was only dimly aware of his arms coming out to catch and hold her as she threw herself against the unexpectedly comforting hardness of his chest.

"What the hell is going on here, Kendra?" he bit out as she buried her face against the slightly damp material of his evening jacket. A part of her mind registered the fact

44

that he must have followed her without going back to his apartment to get his coat.

"I'll explain later," she insisted frantically. "Do something, Case, I think he's dead! I didn't mean to kill him! I only meant to—"

Without a word he disentangled himself from her frantically clinging embrace and set her gently aside.

She watched, appalled, as he went down on one knee beside the fallen man and examined him with quick expertise.

"Is he—"

"He'll be fine," Case cut in brusquely, slanting a speculative, dark glance up at her alarmed features. "What did you do to him, Kendra?"

"I—I threw him. He was coming at me, and I just threw him. I think he hit his head on that set of drawers when he went down, though." Kendra took a deep breath, struggling for control of her shaking voice.

It was all right now. Case would know what to do next. Lord! Who would have thought things would get so complicated? You never worried about what to do after you'd downed your opponent while practicing. You didn't think about things like calling the police, having to fetch a doctor, or coming up with explanations. . . .

"Who is he, Kendra?"

Case's voice seemed suddenly quite hard to her. She glanced from the fallen man to the black-haired, one-eyed man at his side. Case not only sounded hard, he looked hard. Kendra swallowed as her rational faculties finally reasserted themselves. What did she really know about Case Garrett? There was absolutely no reason on earth to view him as a potential ally! This was his town, and he would know all the important people, such as the police and the owner of the hotel where she was staying. His loyalties would be clearly defined, and they wouldn't necessarily include her!

"I—I don't know, Case," she began with greater caution, rapidly sorting through her short list of options. She had her loyalties, too, and it was time she started remembering them. "He was waiting for me in the hall when I came back to my room. Are you sure he's going to be all right?"

"I'm sure," Case remarked with evident lack of interest in that subject. He was reaching for the man's wallet, flipping open the worn leather folder to examine the few cards and papers inside. "His license says his name is Gilbert Phelps. Mean anything to you? He's a private investigator."

"No. Case, do you think we should get him to a doctor? He might have a concussion or something."

"I expect he's had worse in his time," Case retorted dispassionately, stuffing the wallet back into the man's coat pocket and getting to his feet. "But I think it is time we cleaned up the mess."

Wide-eyed, she watched him walk calmly over to the telephone. She licked her dry lower lip anxiously before saying as coolly as possible, "Do you—uh—think it's necessary to call the police?"

He gave her a level look. "I'm not calling the police."

"Oh." She hoped the relief didn't show in her voice. She watched him dial, fascinated.

"Get me Wolf," Case said with quiet authority as someone on the other end answered. He stood easily while he waited, his gaze never leaving Kendra's taut face.

"Wolf, tell Johnny he's in charge for a while. I need you." Rapidly he gave the other man the name of Kendra's hotel and her room number. "No, she's fine," he concluded in response to some question from his assistant. "But at the moment she looks like a woman who may have gotten herself in over her head." He dropped the phone back onto its cradle just as the man on the floor groaned.

Instantly Kendra's attention went back to her uninvited

46

visitor. She stepped closer as Gilbert Phelps stirred painfully and opened his fierce blue eyes. The look he gave her was murderously and frustratedly angry.

Kendra remembered how easy it had been to handle the man, and some of her inner anxiety faded. She ignored Case as she moved to stand staring down at Phelps.

"Did Radburn send you?" she asked quietly.

"What do you think?" Phelps muttered, touching his head with tentative fingers. "I'll get you for this," he went on forcefully, wincing.

"I think there's been enough violence this evening," Case murmured, stepping forward into Gilbert Phelps's line of sight. "Let's not have any more threats."

Phelps jerked in reaction as he realized Kendra was not alone. There was also a sudden look of understanding on his ratlike features. "So you're the one who hit me! What's the matter? Afraid to meet me face to face?" he demanded belligerently.

"I didn't hit you," Case said with dangerous softness, which obviously had an impact on the man. "If I had, you wouldn't be waking up with only a small bump on the head. Now, suppose you answer the lady's question. Or would you rather do your explaining to the police?"

Phelps sat up slowly, his eyes darting rapidly from Case to Kendra. "You won't be calling the cops," he charged. "*She* doesn't want them involved any more than I do!"

Kendra bit her lip to stifle her response, as Case tossed her a quick, silencing glance.

"Miss Loring will follow my advice in the matter," he told Phelps calmly. "And if I instruct her to involve the police, she will do so. Is that clear?"

The man flashed an uneasy look at the quietly threatening man in front of him and obviously decided to try another tactic. "Look, there's no point calling the cops. Nobody's done anything—"

"You think you can explain exactly what you're doing in this room?" Case invited.

"Sure I can! She invited me in!" Gilbert Phelps announced with sudden conviction, making it clear he had decided on his line of defense. "She lured me up here, and then tried to steal my wallet."

"Why, you cheap, two-bit punk!" Kendra exclaimed, infuriated at being unjustly accused.

"That's enough, Kendra," Case told her coolly. "I'll handle this."

Kendra heard the hard metal in his deep voice and found herself obeying. She knew she shouldn't be relinquishing control of the situation to Case, but for the life of her, she wasn't sure how to avoid doing so at that moment. Case seemed very much in charge and likely to remain so.

"You forget, Phelps, the lady has me for a witness. And in this town I can promise you the cops will take my word long before they take yours, especially given the physical evidence. Do you believe me?"

Gilbert Phelps lapsed into a sullen expression that told its own story. "I only wanted to talk to her. Get some information," he muttered.

"For whom?" Case pressed almost gently. Kendra shivered at the tone of his voice and knew it had had an effect on Phelps, too.

"A—a client. Look, I wasn't going to hurt her, dammit, I—"

"Who was paying you for the information?" Case repeated patiently, sitting down on the edge of the bed with a casualness that fooled no one.

"She knows," Phelps snapped.

"It was Radburn?" Kendra breathed.

Phelps shrugged.

"What did Radburn want to know?" Case drawled.

"He thought this lady would know where his wife is,"

Gilbert Phelps admitted harshly. "He paid me to ask her a few questions, that's all." His slitty glance was on Kendra's carefully blank face. "But he didn't pay me enough to get myself into this kind of mess. I just quit!"

"Yes," Case agreed pleasantly, nodding. "You did. Remember that in the future if you're tempted to get back on Radburn's payroll. Because next time I might be tempted to take a more forceful hand in your early retirement. . . ."

There was a quick, hard knock on the door, and Kendra whirled, startled.

"It's all right," Case told her. "That'll be Wolf. Let him in."

Wolf surveyed the scene with a professional eye as Kendra opened the door and stepped aside. "The lady get herself in a bit of trouble, boss?"

"I'm afraid so, Wolf. This gentleman needs to be shown the back door. Would you mind playing the gracious host?"

"Sure, Case," Wolf said, turning to smile soothingly at Kendra as he stepped toward Phelps. The smile had the same sharklike quality Case's had on occasion. Not soothing at all.

"Now, just a minute," Gilbert Phelps began, beginning to sound panicked.

"Don't worry, Wolf won't hurt you, will you, Wolf?"

"Nope," Wolf assured the fallen man cheerfully, reaching down to lift him unceremoniously to his feet. "Not if you behave yourself. Say good-bye to the lady."

Phelps ignored that instruction, contenting himself with a glare instead. At the door, Case stopped both men temporarily with a last reminder.

"You will remember our little discussion, Phelps? You'll vet your potential employers a bit more thoroughly in the future?"

"I'm out of this mess, don't worry," Phelps agreed,

stifling a groan as he touched his tender head. "Radburn doesn't pay enough for this kind of treatment!"

Wolf calmly shut the door behind himself and his new acquaintance. Kendra watched them disappear, her mind churning. She continued to stare blankly at the closed door until Case's words brought her head around with a snap.

"Get your things together, Kendra. I'm taking you home."

"Home!"

"My home," he clarified, his mouth twisting in a grim smile.

"Back to the casino? But I don't want to go back, Case." She waved an all-encompassing hand, indicating the scene in her room. "I appreciate what you did by helping me get rid of Gilbert Phelps, but it doesn't change anything. I'll be leaving first thing in the morning."

"To report back to Donna?" he inquired, one brow lifting slightly.

"It's really none of your business, Case," she told him in a controlled tone, eyeing him intently for a clue as to how involved he planned to get.

"It is now. Pack your suitcase."

She stood her ground, chin lifting. "Who do you think you are to tell me what to do?" she demanded quietly.

"The man who is going to get some answers to questions that were neatly sidestepped earlier this evening." He swung his gaze around the room, spotting the half-packed suitcase at once and heading toward it.

"Don't you dare!" Kendra snapped as he hauled her few items out of the closet and dumped them into the bag. She started forward angrily, not quite certain how she was going to go about stopping him but determined not to let him take over completely.

"Use your head," he growled, not paying any attention to her advance. "As long as Phelps knows where you are,

50

you aren't safe. Or maybe he isn't safe," Case added thoughtfully as he closed and latched the bag. "I don't think he'll be back, but it's conceivable he'll summon up enough guts to call Radburn and tell him what happened."

"Don't be ridiculous! There's nothing more Radburn can do tonight. I'm sure he's still in Los Angeles. And even if he did show up, or send someone else, I can deal with it!"

"Oh, hell," Case gritted, hoisting the suitcase after a last check of the bathroom. "You got lucky one time, and now you think you're the latest thing in avenging amazons!"

"It wasn't luck. It was skill!" she stated proudly. "Put down that suitcase, dammit. I'm not going anywhere!"

"Just watch," he advised succinctly, taking her arm. "Unless of course you want to try some of your tricks on me."

"Listen to me," she pleaded, trying for a rational approach. "Whatever else he is, Radburn isn't a—a hood. He wouldn't really hire someone to hurt me. He just wants some answers." She hoped.

"It sounds like he and I have something in common," Case murmured, propelling her gently but firmly toward the door. "But I prefer to ask my questions in person."

"I'm not going with you tonight, Case—"

"And I don't intend to go back to the casino and worry about you all evening," he countered, softening the words with a smile.

"There's no need to worry," she began, pouncing on the slight gentling in him. "I'll be fine, really."

"Not after I tell the front desk what just happened up here in this room," he retorted silkily.

Kendra whitened. "You wouldn't!"

"I know the owner of this hotel," he went on smoothly. "It will take me about five minutes to convince him he doesn't need you as a guest."

"But I didn't do anything!" she protested, shocked.

"Phelps's story might sound very plausible if I tell it his way—"

"Case!"

"Coming, Kendra?" he asked politely, holding the door.

Floored by the sudden turn of events, Kendra stared at him, open-mouthed. She didn't really fear this man, although perhaps she ought to do so. And she'd just had all the proof she needed that she could handle herself if it came to physical assault. But she wasn't sure at all if he would carry out his implied promise to get her kicked out of the hotel. Common sense told her Case Garrett could make a great deal of trouble for her if he chose. At least in this town. And what if Radburn *were* to send someone else tonight?

"Where will I stay?" she asked suspiciously.

"I have a spare room." He sighed impatiently. "You'll be safe at my place, Kendra."

She considered that, her head tilted to one side as she thought about the various possibilities. Perhaps the easiest thing would be to go along with what he wanted, at least for the moment. It would at least get her out of the hotel room, and the more she thought about Gilbert Phelps running around loose, the more she decided that that might not be a bad idea. Case seemed more concerned with satisfying his curiosity than anything else. She probably would be safe. After all, he certainly hadn't pressed her too much earlier in the evening. But there was one point . . .

"How did you happen to show up so conveniently in my doorway?" she asked as a sudden thought asserted itself. "Did you follow me?"

"You weren't very cooperative when I asked where you were staying," he explained without any sign of apology.

"I *knew* I was being followed!"

"That wasn't me you were aware of. It was probably Phelps," Case told her with great certainty. "We're wasting time, Kendra. Let's go."

She stared at him, debating the merits of further argument. He seemed to have made up his mind and was quite willing to make things uncomfortable for her if she didn't go along. That was the negative side. On the positive side was the fact that she wasn't really concerned about him using physical force against her once she was back in his apartment. And he had been very helpful with the problem of Gilbert Phelps. She was feeling grateful for that.

What it came down to, Kendra knew, was that in spite of his undoubtedly somewhat veiled background, she trusted him. He was making himself difficult and mildly annoying, but she trusted him. She realized he had built that inexplicable sense of trust during dinner earlier in his apartment.

Her head held high, she walked through the door, her graceful stride taking her rapidly down the hushed hall to the elevators. She heard him follow, and when he came up behind her and stabbed the call button, she slanted him a reproachful glance.

"You wouldn't really have made trouble for me with the management, would you?" It was more of a statement than a question.

"I make it a point not to use more force than a situation calls for," he replied coolly.

"That doesn't answer my question."

"It should. Think about it."

"You're upset with me, aren't you?" she demanded in surprise as they descended to the lobby.

"Upset is a rather mild word for my current mood," he drawled laconically.

She arched an eyebrow quellingly. "There's no justification for that sort of attitude. You barely even know me. What happened here tonight is certainly none of your business. I think you're annoyed because you can't figure out what's going on."

She smiled knowingly as she concluded her statement, and his expression hardened.

"Knocking poor Phelps unconscious has certainly put a sparkle in your eye," he observed unkindly. "Or at least it did once you realized you hadn't killed him. Do you do this sort of thing a lot?"

"Only when necessary," she told him in liquid accents. He was right, she thought. Her success in defending herself against Phelps had given her a strange kind of high. She could still feel the adrenaline flowing, although the surging energy had faded. She felt jubilant, exultant, very sure of herself. She couldn't wait to tell her instructor. That thought curved her lips even further in utter satisfaction.

"Feel like you could take on the world, hmmm? Is that why you're not making too much of a fuss about coming home with me? You think you can handle me?"

She wanted to laugh but managed to refrain. Her eyes gleamed with the emotion, however, as she looked up at him. "You did me a favor tonight. And I know you're curious. I suppose I can give you a few answers in return. Also, you may have a point about Phelps. If he found me this evening, it's conceivable someone else could do the same. I would just as soon not have to keep entertaining uninvited guests. That sort of thing could get tiring. Besides, something tells me I'll be quite safe at your place."

"It doesn't do much for a man's ego to have a woman tell him she considers him safe," he said dryly as the elevator opened and they stepped out into the lobby.

"It's been my experience that most men don't need any extra boost for their egos."

No one paid them any attention as they walked out the front door and hailed a cab for the return trip. It occurred to Kendra that Case must have been freezing without a topcoat, but he seemed to ignore the weather. She noticed with amusement that he took her into the casino via another entrance, however, and wondered if it was his own reputation he was trying to protect. He certainly couldn't be concerned about hers. No one here knew her or would ever see her again.

"Now, what are you laughing to yourself about?" he inquired as he ushered her back to his apartment.

"I was thinking about how you're sneaking me in here," she grinned cheerfully as he opened the door to the tropical fantasy room. "Worried someone will see you with my suitcase and get the wrong impression?"

"It did strike me that the fewer people who saw you enter, the better. Unless you have some way of knowing for certain that Phelps was working alone," he shot back irritably, shutting the heavy door with a small slam.

She sent a humorous glance back over the white fur on her shoulder, saw his set features, and shook her head ruefully. "To tell you the truth, I don't know how far Radburn would really go. That's one of the reasons I took you up on your kind offer."

He regarded her steadily for a few seconds, and then started toward the hall. She followed curiously.

"For the record," he stated very clearly as he led her into a bedroom and tossed her suitcase down on a wide bed, "I never do anything out of kindness."

"I suppose the motivating force in this case is plain, old curiosity, isn't it?" she murmured absently, taking in the bedroom furnishings.

The tropical motif had been carried out here, too, with a lavish hand. The all-white, quilted bed had an elaborate wicker screen for a headboard. The furniture was rattan, and the wall hangings were silk-screen prints of fabulous South Sea flowers in glowing colors. The woven grass mats had been interspersed with thick white carpet, and one wall was mirrored. Large potted plants stood like green sculptures in the corners.

"This is your room," Kendra exclaimed before he could respond to her first remark. "You said you had a spare room for me!"

"Don't look so accusing. There is a spare room. I'll be using it."

"Oh." She eyed him narrowly. "That's not necessary, you know. I don't want to make you go to all that trouble."

Something warmed briefly in his dark gaze. "You're inviting me to spend the night in here with you?"

"Don't be ridiculous!"

"I was afraid you'd say that." He sighed. He glanced around. "Well, suppose you take your coat off and get settled in. When you're ready come out into the living room, and we'll have our little talk."

"The story really isn't all that interesting, you know," she warned.

"I'm sure I'll be fascinated."

She watched him walk out, an amused smile playing lightly around her lips. The physical high of the excitement of her encounter with Phelps was still clinging. She didn't mind the thought of giving Case Garrett a few answers. She wanted, no, *needed* to talk to someone for a while. She needed to let the bubbling sensation settle down before she tried sleeping. A disinterested party like Case, who had no connection with the whole affair, seemed ideal. Perhaps that was the real reason she'd allowed him to bring her back to his apartment.

She heard the knock on the apartment door a few minutes later but paid no attention when she heard Wolf's low tones. She hung up her coat and was rehanging the dress she planned to wear on the airplane back to San Francisco when she realized Case had taken his assistant into the study.

56

There was an expensive look about Case Garrett's wardrobe, Kendra reflected as she made room for her few things. But she supposed a casino owner had to keep up appearances. Slipping out of her sandals, which were beginning to hurt her feet, she finished her few chores and padded quietly down the hall toward the living room.

The study door was open only a fraction of an inch as she walked past, but she could hear Case's electrifying words. In an instant her sparkling, almost effervescent mood was shattered.

"You took care of Phelps?"

"He won't be giving Miss Loring any more trouble," Wolf vowed softly, with the sound of a man who has performed similar tasks satisfactorily in the past.

"Did you get anything out of him?" Case persisted calmly.

Kendra felt abruptly chilled. What, exactly, had Wolf Higgins done to that poor man? Phelps had, after all, only been a paid agent of Radburn's! And it wasn't as if the slimy little man had pulled a knife or a gun on her! He had only been intending to scare some answers out of her.

She hesitated a few inches from the door, not certain if she wanted to hear any more.

"I don't think he knows much, boss," Wolf said. "He didn't seem to know anything about Radburn, except by name. The guy paid him to hassle Miss Loring and get some answers about his wife—"

"Donna Radburn?"

"Yeah."

"How much did he know about Kendra?" Case inquired deliberately.

Kendra shivered as Wolf replied coolly, "She's out of San Francisco. He followed her here to Lake Tahoe on a plane yesterday."

"Which means he probably followed her here tonight," Case concluded thoughtfully.

Wolf said nothing, letting the obvious speak for itself. There was a silence in the study, and Kendra drew a long, steadying breath, backing silently toward the bedroom.

Something was wrong. Case Garrett wasn't acting like a gallant gentleman. He was getting far too involved for that. Quite suddenly all her initial qualms about the man returned in full force. She was being a fool to trust him. Hadn't he just told her himself he never did anything out of kindness?

The two men in the study had sounded cold and professional in a way that tore the sparkling exhilaration of the evening to pieces. And the way Case had begun inquiring into her personal background was more than a little unnerving. What was going on here? Was there more to Donna's gambling debt than the other woman had admitted?

Her instincts telling her it was time to move, Kendra made her way on silent, nylon-covered feet back to the bedroom, grabbed her purse and shoes, and turned toward the door.

It was a shame to leave all her things behind, but a feeling of urgency was riding her now. She wanted out of the fantasy before she got swallowed up in it again. She would need her coat, and it was much too expensive to leave behind.

Holding her sandals in one hand, coat and purse in the other, she slipped quietly back down the hall, passing the study and shuddering a little. Wolf was still closeted with his boss, and she caught the serious overtones of the discussion as she went past. They were talking about her, she knew.

Moving like a wraith in a manner that was instinctive after two years of training, Kendra made her way through the living room into the entrance hall. She had a momentary feeling of panic as she opened the door, and then she was through it. The elevator seemed to take forever, but at last she was safely inside. In another few minutes she would be safe. She would go to another hotel for the night, use a different name.

She was thinking clearly by the time she exited the elevator, and she decided to use the back entrance through which Case had brought her earlier. The fewer people who witnessed her departure, the better.

She breathed a sigh of thankful relief when the doorknob was finally under her trembling fingers. Desperately grateful for the streak of good luck, she flung it open—and walked straight into the solid brick wall that was Wolfgang Amadeus Higgins.

"Oh!"

Automatically her hand came up to brace herself.

"Wolf! What are you doing here? I thought—"

"You thought he was upstairs, Kendra?"

She whirled at the sound of Case's lazy, amused drawl. "There are other ways out of this building besides the elevator. Wolf and I used one when we realized you were ducking out on our hospitality."

Kendra fought the fear that had sprung alive in the pit of her stomach. These men were dangerous, and she was way out of her league. She saw the cool threat in Case and shivered. Feminine intuition told her there was no mercy to be had there. She turned to Wolf.

"Please let me pass, Wolf," she ordered haughtily. "I want to leave."

His battered face looked incredibly sad and apologetic. "I'm sorry, Miss Loring," he said, sounding it. "But Case, here, wants to talk to you."

"And what Case wants matters more than what I want?" she challenged, knowing the answer.

"I'm afraid so, ma'am." He sighed regretfully.

She gritted her teeth, refusing to give into the panic. Her eyes locked with Wolf's rueful but determined gaze, and then she turned on her bare heels, her shoes still in her hand.

Not deigning to speak, she brushed past the elegantly menacing man standing in the doorway and walked back to the elevator. The whole casino was a trap, she finally acknowledged, feeling incredibly stupid. Case Garrett owned everyone and everything in it.

Without a word he ushered her back into the elevator, leaving Wolf behind in the hall.

Staring straight ahead as Case once again opened the door to the apartment, Kendra gathered her courage to ask evenly, "If I give you the answers you want tonight, Case, will you let me go?"

"No," he said mildly, "I don't think so, Kendra. You'll be staying until morning."

CHAPTER FOUR

"You have no right to do this," Kendra began in an almost conversational voice as she sank into the pillows of the sofa and crossed her legs with casual grace. "But, then, you already know that, don't you?"

Case poured a brandy for each of them and brought her a snifter before sitting down across from her in a rattan lounging chair. He smiled silkily. He was making very little effort to shield the hardness in himself now, she realized. It was as if he had accepted the fact that she knew his true nature, and he didn't intend to waste any more time hiding it.

But the female instinct in her picked up on something else in that cool, calculating gaze. He still wanted her.

A tremor went through her as she forced herself to review the potential of that fact.

"It seems to me that after the favor I did for you this evening, you could accept my hospitality a little more graciously," he said.

"I might have done exactly that," she admitted recklessly, "if I thought that was all that was involved. But I heard you talking to Wolf in the study. . . ."

"It occurred to me you might have overheard us." He smiled at her apologetically. "You didn't think too highly of my personal integrity when you originally appeared in the casino this evening, and although you stopped worrying about it somewhat over dinner, all the accusations were back in your eyes when you found Wolf and I waiting for you downstairs."

"Do you blame me? I've got a rather delicate situation on my hands right now. I don't need further complications."

"What sort of complications are you worried about, Kendra?" he murmured pointedly.

"This isn't any of your business, Case," she whispered firmly.

"You made it my business when you walked into the casino tonight."

"No!"

He dismissed her protest with a flat, arcing movement of his hand. "And now, having helped you—uh—dispose of that little complication back in the hotel room . . ."

"I never asked you to help! You should never have followed me!" she snapped.

"But I did, and I couldn't miss the relief in your face when you looked up and saw me in the doorway. You quite willingly turned everything over to me at that point, didn't you? Why don't you stop fighting your instincts and do the same again? Tell me what this is all about, Kendra. How are you involved with the Radburns?"

"Why do you care?" she charged softly, her bare foot swinging in an unconscious display of nerves. How badly did he want her? Could she work on it? Make him think first of satisfying his desire for her and postponing this discussion? Kendra had never deliberately set out to seduce a man in her life. She wasn't sure she could do it now, especially given the strained circumstances.

"Let's just say I have a stake in the matter." His gaze flickered over the shape of her leg as she moved slightly. Then he let it trail upward, lingering for a few burning seconds on the rise and fall of her breast beneath the red silk before meeting her eyes.

"Because of the money Donna owes you? You'll get it. Don't worry."

"I intend to," he agreed, taking a sip of his brandy. "Now talk. Tell me about the Radburns."

She shrugged. "There's not much to tell. They're in the process of getting a divorce."

"Then why is Radburn trying to track down his wife?"

"He doesn't want the divorce. It's that simple."

"He can't bear to lose her?" There was dry mockery in his words. Kendra had the feeling Case Garrett found it hard to understand how any man might feel so intensely about a woman.

"He can't bear to lose the money she inherits in a couple of months when she turns twenty-seven." Her voice was cold, remote.

"I see. That makes more sense."

She heard the satisfaction in him and silently gritted her teeth. Of course such an explanation would make perfect sense to him.

"And what's your role in all this? Why are you running errands for Donna and trying to help her hide from Radburn?" he probed relentlessly.

"Donna is my cousin," she told him shortly, refusing to volunteer anything else.

He nodded. "Why is it necessary for Donna to hide? Has Radburn threatened her?"

A corner of Kendra's mouth lifted in disgust. "You saw that little weasel he sent after me. What do you think?"

"Why doesn't she go to the police?" he asked reasonably.

"There's . . . someone else involved." The words came slowly.

"Who?"

"Donna has a son. If Austin Radburn gets his hands on the boy, he can force Donna to return. She's got custody, but that wouldn't mean much if Austin managed to get hold of Jason. He could make Donna do just about anything with that sort of leverage."

"Like come back to him and bring her inheritance with her?" Case hazarded grimly.

"Exactly." She lifted her head, eyeing him narrowly. "And that, in a nutshell, is that. End of story. As you can see, it really has nothing to do with you. May I go now?"

"In the morning," he told her absently, his thoughts clearly elsewhere.

"Case, I don't want to stay."

"I make you nervous?" His mouth twisted in a crooked imitation of a smile.

"Frankly, yes."

"You have nothing to fear," he soothed, his voice dropping to a deeper, warming note that made her even more tense. "You're safe here."

She shut her eyes in a small, frustrated movement, and then gave him a direct look. "I don't feel safe here."

"You're afraid I'll force myself on you?" he asked softly.

She blinked, startled. "Of course not," she told him quickly.

He hesitated, and then said probingly, "No . . . you're not physically afraid of me, are you? You weren't afraid of Phelps tonight, either. Merely concerned that you might have seriously hurt him. You're one very self-confident woman, Kendra Loring. As I told you before, you intrigue me."

"Is your pet wolf still guarding the door?" she inquired acidly, ignoring his words.

"All night long," he assured her gently. "You may as well relax. You're not going anywhere."

"I've satisfied your curiosity," she reminded him pointedly.

"But I'm not satisfied you'll be safe tonight if I send you

out into the streets. I'm going to keep you here and then see you safely on the plane in the morning."

"Against my wishes?"

"It needn't be that way," he said meaningfully.

Kendra picked up the sexual innuendo and once again considered that approach. Slowly, invitingly, she smiled at him.

"Meaning?"

"You know what I mean," he said calmly. But she could almost feel the sensual heat in his gaze. If Case were not around, Wolf could be handled, her agile mind reflected. The big man couldn't watch all the exits. She could mingle with the crowd in the casino, leave with a large group . . .

"Are you thinking of making me more resigned to my—er—fate?" she taunted.

"Is this how you lured poor Phelps to his doom this evening?" Case asked, ending with a note of soft male laughter. "Did you smile at him like that and invite him into your room, then bop him on the head?"

"Not quite. He didn't wait for an invitation, you see."

"Unlike me?"

"Are you waiting for one?"

"Perhaps," he growled seductively. He got to his feet, setting down his brandy and coming to stand in front of her.

She sat very still, a faint smile on her lips as he drank in the sight of her lounging on his sofa. The masculine anticipation in the dark gaze was doing funny things to her insides, but she summoned up all her will to ignore the effects. What happened next would have to be handled with a clear head, or it could end in disaster.

"Are you issuing the invitation, Kendra?" he rasped huskily, taking her hand and lifting her lightly to her feet beside him.

She felt the tension of male desire in him, knew beyond

a doubt that he wanted her. A man was weak when he was in the throes of sexual desire, she told herself.

Her lashes fluttered down onto her cheek, and she lifted her face for his kiss.

"I thought you might," he congratulated himself hoarsely. "You wanted me earlier this evening, didn't you?" He lowered his head slowly, his thumb probing the edge of her slightly parted lips with a sensuousness that seeped into her bloodstream. He didn't wait for a verbal answer. "As badly as I wanted you, I wonder?"

She let him take her lips, her arms sliding around his neck as he fastened his mouth on hers with controlled passion. There was no denying his expertise, she thought distantly.

But she had kissed other men who had definite expertise. Case Garrett's embrace was different, more direct somehow. More electric.

She tried to put the surprising depth of her own reaction aside and concentrate on arousing him. She needed to get him well beyond this point of control. He wanted her, but he had his emotions on a tight leash. She needed him to be weakened with desire, not merely attracted to her.

"We're going to be very good together, Kendra Loring," he grated against her mouth, and then his hands were going around her, pulling her close. "I knew that the moment I saw you this evening."

"Did you?" she breathed, aware of her quickening pulse and striving to conquer it. Surely there was no possibility of her losing her self-control! Not with this man!

"Ummm." He began to shower soft, feathery kisses along her cheek while his fingers spread against her slender back. "I had to follow you back to that hotel. I couldn't just let you walk out of my life having received only a few kisses. Not when I knew there could be so much more between us!"

She heard the deepening tone of his voice and smiled to

herself. Her fingertips toyed with the blackness of his hair, and she temporarily gave in to the curiously light-headed sensation his embrace was creating. Soon she would be able to act, but in the meantime . . . .

"Oh . . . !"

She heard the low, half-stifled moan and was startled to realize it had come from her own throat. Involuntarily her hands tightened on the muscles of his shoulders, and her body arched willingly beneath the pressure of his hands.

Case gave a deep exclamation of spiraling desire and satisfaction at her response. His fingers slid down to her hips, holding her more tightly against him. Kendra sucked in her breath, realizing he wanted her to be totally aware of his need. She felt the hardness in him and trembled when he traced the line of her spine up to the sensitive nape of her neck.

"Case?" His name was a gentle, beseeching sound, and in that moment Kendra could not have said whether the feminine plea was deliberate or instinctive on her part.

He smiled against her cheek, his fingers gliding inside the collar of her dress. Then she shivered again as his warm tongue circled the perimeter of her ear and then stabbed excitingly inside.

When he felt her response his hands went to her hair, prying at the gold clip with rising urgency.

"My God! A man could get lost in this stuff," he muttered as the multicolored brown mass tumbled to her waist. He twined his hands in it, lifting the sweet-smelling hair and burying his face in it for a long, sensuous moment.

Kendra gasped, struggling to maintain her grip on reality and her own plans. It was astonishing how this man's growing desire struck a resonant chord deep in her body. It had never been quite like this with anyone else. For the first time in two years she began wondering if her needs had returned to normal after the trauma. For the past two years she had been perfectly content with a little mild affection, a few kisses . . .

But tonight there was a strange curiosity coursing along her nerve endings. It tempted her in a way that went beyond the normal level of desire she had known before the incident two years ago. This man was different, her body declared with absolute conviction. This man was *right*!

No, she told herself wildly, fighting the battle she knew she must win. This man was not right. She needed to get away from him, perhaps more than ever now. Too much was at stake. . . .

"You have the nicest hands," he rasped, turning his head to touch his tongue to the inside of her wrist. "Light, gentle, exquisite. I like the feel of them on me."

"Do you, Case?" she managed breathlessly, striving to keep her wits about her as the rush hit her.

"Yes," he told her huskily. "Touch me some more, little mystery lady. Forget about the past and the future and just touch me again and again tonight!"

Her hands slid down his jacket front, and she eased it off his broad shoulders, telling herself that she was only putting on an act, doing what was necessary to get herself safely away from him.

The elegantly tailored coat fell unheeded to the floor, and she lifted trembling fingers to the black bow tie, pulling it free. It followed the coat, and she felt his pleasure.

And then she felt something else—the feel of his hands on her zipper. The action penetrated her swimming thoughts, producing a warning. She would not be able to flee, naked, into the night, she reminded herself grimly. She must do what had to be done before he had undressed her!

"Wait," she whispered softly, lightly capturing his hands and pulling them around in front of her so that she could drop tiny kisses on his fingers. "Wait a little while."

"Why?" he asked deeply, spreading his fingertips out to touch her face as she caressed them. "Why must I wait? We both know what we want."

"Wouldn't you—wouldn't you like to have me finish what I've started first?" she suggested, her breath catching in her throat as she lifted her eyes to meet the full impact of his sensual look.

There was a new kind of hardness in his face, she thought distractedly. A taut, tense expression of masculine need. The kind of need that would make him unable to think of anything else except getting her into bed. She was sure of it.

"You want to finish undressing me before I return the favor?" he smiled whimsically.

"Do you mind?"

"No," he murmured, taking her hand and leading her toward the bedroom. "I have no objections whatsoever. You're an amazing woman, do you know that? I'm glad you're not going to insist on being coy. I'm grateful you're capable of being honest about what you want."

She found herself leaning heavily against his side, his arm wrapped around her waist as he led her down the hall.

"What about you, Case? Do you want me?"

"More than you can possibly guess," he confessed a little grimly as he stopped beside the bed.

"It's—it's easy for a man to want a woman on sight, isn't it?" she whispered, her shaking fingers going to the buttons of his shirt.

"Yes," he admitted. "But this is different. You're different. . . ." He kissed her ear, her throat, the back of her neck, as she tugged at his shirt.

"I don't believe that," she told him on a thread of sound. "I think you've done this a thousand times."

"Gone to bed with a woman so soon after meeting her? No, Kendra, I haven't done it a thousand times. What about you? Do you always know what you want so quickly?"

She slid his shirt off him, and her fingers went at once to the curling hair that covered his chest. He was built like the jungle cat he resembled, she thought fleetingly. Lean, graceful, hard.

"No," she said, a horrifying nervousness assailing her as the final seconds closed in on her. She would have to act quickly, and she had never felt less coordinated or less ready for that action. Her body was threatening to betray her, and part of her problem was her mind's inability to accept the betrayal. He was only another man. A man she could handle. What was the matter with her?

"No? There is no man waiting for you back in San Francisco?" he persisted heavily as she traced the outline of his male nipples. She felt him catch his breath and knew he was going rapidly beyond the point of control. It was all she could do to control herself now. She had to make her move.

"If I said there was, would you change your mind about tonight?" she asked thickly.

He hesitated, and then groaned his answer in an implacable, uncompromising whisper.

"Nothing could make me change my mind about tonight. If there *is* another man, the only thing I can think about right now is making you forget him!"

Kendra took hold of herself, sensing the moment was at hand. In another few seconds he would be reaching out for her, pulling her down onto the white quilt, and then she would be lost. She knew that with sudden, brilliant clarity, and the knowledge both attracted and repelled.

She stepped gracefully, easily out of reach, flashing a smile of invitation.

"Kendra?" Sensual menace flickered in his dark gaze, and then he was reaching for her, his hand seeking her to draw her close again.

70

God! She would have to be fast. The fall would have to stun him long enough to give her sufficient time to escape.

She caught at his extended hand, forcing herself to let the trained reactions of her body take over. She must see him as attacker, not lover!

It was going to be easy, she thought with a surge of charged energy. He was expecting nothing like this. He was off-balance and consumed with desire. If ever a man was vulnerable . . .

When his hand descended she stepped back slightly and felt him adjust automatically to her slight change in balance. Once again she stepped back, sliding her left foot in an arc to the rear. She shifted her weight, feeling him follow the gentle lead until he was caught by her ankle. In a split second she moved, pulling his arm in an upward circular motion with her right hand and using her left hand in a downward circular motion. The throw was completed by bringing him over her foot, and she concluded it perfectly, her left knee properly bent, her waist straight and firm.

As soon as he hit the rug she knew she had made a mistake. He didn't fall like a dead weight. He wasn't stunned by the impact. He landed with the trained reflexes she would have expected from a master such as her instructor!

There was barely time to assimilate the error before his hand struck out to catch her ankle. Shocked, Kendra tried to fight free, wanting to kick at him but unable to do so. Frantically she tried to remember her instruction, but she had never considered this possibility. She had expected to have all the advantages of surprise.

Belatedly she began to recall some of the art, but everything was happening much too fast. With a savage yank she was jerked off her feet. Kendra managed to break her fall in the proper manner but was unable to recover in time to retaliate.

Case was on her then, his face a cold mask of fury and desire. A deadly combination that she felt the force of as if the wind had been knocked out of her. And then she began fighting, calling on everything she had learned in the past two years.

It was a silent, bitter, savage battle, and she was losing it. Worse, every attack or defense she used was angering Case further. But it was not a white-hot, burning anger that might have left him vulnerable. Case was all icy, controlled wrath.

Beneath the impact of his superior skill, Kendra felt herself succumbing to panic. She began to flail at him in useless feminine ways, using her nails on his face until he caught her hands and anchored them. She kicked at his legs but missed the target. She writhed and twisted, as he pinned her inevitably into the white carpet, exhausting herself with panic and fear.

Neither of them said a word during the struggle, and it was somehow all the more violent for being carried out in silence. It ended as she had known it would end the moment she realized she had taken on more than she could handle.

Helpless, damp with perspiration and fear, the red silk dress torn, she finally went still beneath Case's weight. Wide-eyed, she watched his taut face, seeing no possibility of mercy in the roughly hewn features.

She lay panting, unable to move, waiting for him to hurt her. It was all she could do not to cry out in fear and pain. Her mind was flashing wildly, horribly back to that night two years ago when she had once before been at the mercy of a man. She wanted to scream, cry, plead. And in her terror, none of those was possible. She could only lie there, glaring her helpless hatred up at a stone-faced, cold man who now wanted only vengeance.

"You little cheat!" he snarled. "What the hell were you

trying to pull? Or do you go around doing this to men all the time?"

In the utter shock of the moment, Kendra couldn't even manage to speak. She waited mutely for what would come next, summoning all the shattered remains of her poor strength in an effort not to cry. If she could deny him nothing else, she could deny him that satisfaction. Men like this wanted to see women broken and crying.

"Answer me, damn you!" he blazed, his fingers digging into her arms as he held her immobile. "How many times have you done this sort of thing? How many men have fallen for it? Is that really what happened to Phelps this evening? My God! I was only joking earlier when I asked if you'd lured him into your room and then hit him on the head! But that's probably exactly what happened! What were you going to do? Roll him for his wallet?"

"No!" The single word was torn from her in protest. She shut her eyes against the fury in him.

"If it's money you want, you can damn well earn it! But don't think you're going to cheat me out of what you were promising a few minutes ago! I always get what I pay for!"

She was shaking now as she realized there was no hope of reasoning with him. How could she have been so stupid? Why hadn't she even thought about the risks of failure? Why in heaven's name had she been so crazily self-confident? But Phelps had been so easy to deal with! Who would have guessed Case Garrett wouldn't be as simple to handle, especially with his energies directed only toward getting her into bed?

But now that single-minded determination had taken on the aura of primitive male violence and revenge. The sophisticated passion he had been employing only a short time ago was gone, wiped out as if it had never existed.

Kendra's teeth sank into her lower lip, drawing blood, and her nails curled savagely into her palms as she felt his hand on her dress. The peculiar, exotic sound made by silk when it is torn vibrated through the room as the fabric was ripped from her in a quick, fierce motion.

She felt him hurl his few remaining garments into a corner without weakening the painful hold he had on her. An instant later they were both lying naked on the thick white carpet.

With mounting anger and humiliation Kendra understood that Case wasn't even going to lift her onto the bed. He was going to take her there on the floor.

CHAPTER FIVE

Her only defense now lay in withdrawing into a far corner of her mind—a corner from which she could view the attack on her body as if it were happening to a limp and lifeless doll. Frantically she corralled her screaming, jabbering, witless senses and fought to pull them back under control; to hide them in that remote part of her brain.

A part of her registered the success of the retreat by the rigidity of her body. She was aware of the hard, hair-roughened thigh along hers, and she knew of the strength in the sinewy arm across her vulnerable throat, but she forced her mind away from those facts.

Case's hand moved down the length of her naked body, gliding harshly over the tips of her breasts, the small curve of her stomach, and down over her hips. There was no tenderness in his touch, only a fierce need to explore the territory he was going to conquer.

"What's the matter with you?" he taunted hoarsely. "Open your eyes and look at me, dammit! You started this, and now you're going to find out what it's like to finish what you start! How many men would give their right arms to have you where I have you now? For how many men will I be the instrument of revenge? Answer me, damn you!"

Hiding in that far corner of her mind, Kendra tried to focus on only the things she would do when it was all over. For somehow, somewhere, there would be a reckoning.

She would not let another male do this to her and walk away with laughter in his uncaring eyes.

"Open your eyes!"

When she again refused to heed the command his hard thigh was shoved violently between her legs, eliciting an unwilling gasp of pain from her.

"Look at me! I want to see the expression in those lying eyes when you learn that you can't treat men as if they're toys to play with and discard!"

His mouth came down on hers, grinding the soft flesh against her teeth in a way that drew more blood from the wound she had already made in her own lips.

"What the hell have you done to yourself?" he grated, and she knew he had tasted the blood that was already on her mouth. "You don't have to create any self-inflicted damage," he jeered. "I'll be glad to do it for you!"

She could still feel pain, she thought wildly. She hadn't retreated far enough yet. She needed to find an even more remote corner in which to hide. She sought for it, dragging her rapidly numbing senses into an even more distant place until she could no longer feel the sting of her mouth or the overwhelming strength in the lean, masculine body covering hers so completely.

She heard a savage oath muttered against her cheek and wondered why her tormentor didn't get on with his assault. What was slowing him down? Did he want to drag it out purposely in hopes of increasing her humiliation? Her exhausted body was taking in oxygen with short, light pants. She felt crushed under the full weight of Case's frame.

His mouth moved again on her cheek, and she sensed a new annoyance in him.

"Damn it to hell! First blood and now tears! What's the matter, Kendra? Can't you take what you dish out so easily?"

Crying? No, she couldn't be crying! Violently she lashed

76

out at the renegade emotion, dragging it back into hiding with the others. The tears stopped.

"That's better! I'm not so weak as to be swayed by that old trick." His lips were on her throat now, his hands holding her still, pressing her down into the rug. She knew he had forced a way between her legs, was aware of the surging power of his body. In another moment . . .

His hands moved, releasing their grip on her arms and framing her face between rough palms.

"Look at me, Kendra," he ordered again. "Open your eyes and look at me, or I swear to God I'll—"

She didn't wait for the threat. There was no point. Her drooping lashes fluttered open, and she stared up at him, not really seeing the harsh lines of his face. Instead she focused blindly on an imaginary point beyond his dark head.

He swore again and then moved her head from side to side with a shocking gentleness.

"Where the hell are you?" he whispered violently. "What are you doing to yourself?"

She heard the new, rasping uncertainty in his voice, but she didn't respond to it. She was responding to nothing. She was safe, hidden away, waiting for the end.

His thumbs moved to the corners of her mouth, stroking in slow, urgent circles. He groaned heavily, a sound from deep within his chest.

"Stop it! Kendra, listen to me! It's all right now. I'm not going to hurt you!"

She wondered vaguely at the compelling demand in his hoarse words.

"Relax," he went on, the slow, stroking movement of his thumbs widening into larger circles. "Relax, honey. It's okay, everything's okay. You picked a real sucker this time, didn't you? I'm probably the first guy ever to get you at his mercy, and I haven't got the guts to go through with it!"

What was he talking about? Why wasn't he raping her? It's what he had intended when he threw her down on the floor. She knew it was what he had intended!

But he kept talking to her, his voice dark, deep, strangely soothing. It called to the senses she had hidden away, urging them to come back out in the open again. Urging them to trust him. She knew she shouldn't obey, and she tried to restrain her reaction to the calming tone. But her response to it went beyond the rational.

"Please, honey, just relax. I won't hurt you. No one's going to hurt you. I'll take care of everything. You're going to be all right. You're safe. Safe . . ."

His hands kept moving over her, gently chafing her cold, damp skin back to life. He eased his weight but didn't break the physical contact. Case touched his lips lightly, gently to her temples, her cheek, her throat.

They weren't sensual kisses, but quieting, gentling caresses that made no threats. Gradually Kendra returned to her body. Her eyes focused once again, seeing the drawn, tense face of the man above her. She felt, really felt, the warmth in him as he lay against her. The stroking of his fingers down her throat, along her arm, out to her wrist finally penetrated.

"It's okay, honey. I swear, everything's okay. . . ."

"Case?" She could barely manage to utter his name, and when she did it was only a breath of sound containing all the questioning uncertainty that was beginning to consume her as she spiraled back to a semblance of normality.

His mouth twisted wryly as he met her eyes directly at last. "That's a neat trick," he drawled sardonically, but she could hear the faint quiver in his words. "Even better than the first one. You had me scared there for a minute. You're a very clever woman, Kendra Loring. And I'm a fool."

He sat up slowly, watching her face with an assessing glance. She had the impression he was striving to maintain a remote, disgusted air, but he couldn't hide the remnants of his concern.

"Case . . ." Kendra's voice was shaky but returning to full control as she realized she was safe. "Case, I'm sorry. I—I only wanted to go free. I didn't want to stay here with you, and I—I couldn't think of any other way to get out of this place."

She knew he was watching her profile as she focused on the carpet. She sat up nervously and reached for the scrap of red silk to hold in front of her. She forced herself to meet his single-eyed gaze again, flinching from the overpowering intensity of that dark look.

"So you deliberately let me think you wanted to go to bed with me, and then tried to put me out of commission with something as simple as that throw. And I let you sucker me the whole way, didn't I?"

"Hardly," she bit back sadly. "I—I never stood a chance. I knew that the minute I saw you take the fall." She looked away, shame creeping like a red tide into her cheeks.

"How much training have you had?" He sounded austerely curious.

"Almost two years," she admitted.

He said something short and explicit. "And how many men have you used your vast expertise on?" he taunted coldly.

"Gilbert Phelps was the first person I've ever really tried it on." She glanced at him quickly, anxiously. "I didn't lure him into my hotel room, Case. He was at the door when I turned around to close it. He—he said he wanted some answers, and I told him to leave or I'd call the front desk. He tried to grab me. Everything happened so quickly after that. He walked right into the throw. I was going to run out of the room and get some help but he—he didn't get back up. I thought I might have really hurt him, and I was beginning to panic when you showed up at the door."

He waited a moment, and she had to glance away again from his unself-consciously nude body. The smooth muscles of his back curved and rippled sensually beneath his tanned skin. He was sitting with his knees drawn up, his arms draped thoughtfully around them as he surveyed her.

"So after two years of training you got lucky in your first real fight. No wonder you were looking so pleased with yourself. After you realized you hadn't committed murder, that is," he added chidingly.

She flushed again. She *had* been pleased with herself. She couldn't deny it. After two years she had finally thought she had proof that she could take care of herself, that no man would ever again be able to use his superior strength against her. She remembered the adrenaline high she had experienced all the way back to the casino, and she closed her eyes in mortification.

"After Phelps, I must have looked like easy prey, hmmm? After all, I wasn't even trying to attack you. I was only asking you to go to bed with me. The ludicrous part is that I thought you really wanted to do it, too! You're a hell of a good actress, Kendra. I could have sworn you were as turned on as I was!"

He made a small sound of total self-derision. "I've usually got much better instincts about people than that, believe it or not!"

She licked her lower lip, tasting the salty blood. Her mouth was going to be badly bruised by morning. And she had done it to herself. Case hadn't hurt her. For some idiotic reason she found herself wanting to soothe his male ego. Stupid, really. Case Garrett didn't need any reassurance. Nevertheless she heard herself saying hesitantly, "It's—it's not your fault. I was enjoying myself. You're— that is, I'm sure you're a very good lover. . . ."

"Thanks!" He sounded more irritated than ever.

Kendra gritted her teeth. This was coming out all wrong. "But you see, you would have found me just as much of a cheat in the end even if I hadn't been plotting to escape."

"Now, what the hell are you talking about?" he grated.

"I wouldn't have gone to bed with you, Case. I—I don't like sex." The words came out baldly and with devastating honesty.

He stared at her. "You don't like it? You just said you'd been enjoying the preliminaries!"

"That's the only part I enjoy," she explained stonily, wishing she'd never begun the explanation. "A few kisses, a little affection. I'm human enough to want some of the warmth."

"But not the total commitment, is that it?" He reached out and caught her chin with his hand, forcing her to look at him. His eye narrowed as he saw the faint trembling of her bruised mouth.

"That's a funny word for a man to use," she tried to say lightly. "Men don't think of going to bed with a woman as any kind of commitment. At its best, it's more like recreation for them."

"And at its worst?" he probed.

"At its worst, it's what almost happened between us just now."

"Rape."

"Yes." She stared at him unflinchingly.

"How long ago were you raped, Kendra?" he growled softly.

She started, blinking rapidly to recover herself. "Case, I—"

"How long?" he repeated more gently but with total determination.

"I don't discuss it. Not with anyone!"

"Then it's time you did. How long ago did it happen, Kendra?"

"Two years ago." She shut her eyes, feeling helpless even though he was only holding her very lightly by the chin.

He swore very softly, very meaningfully. "Was he ever caught?"

She shook her head, aware of tears beneath her lids once again. Twice in one night? And she hadn't cried at all in almost two full years.

"Do you know his name? Do you know who it was?"

There was nothing but the icy edge of cold steel in his words. The kind of steel used to make swords, Kendra thought, a new fear springing to life in the pit of her stomach.

"I know." She didn't offer anything further, wanting to end the conversation and not knowing how to do so.

"I'll kill him for you." There was no emotion at all in him now.

"Case! Don't say that!" Her eyes flew open, the hazel gaze glistening with moisture. She caught his hand in a frantic movement. "You don't even know me! For God's sake! A few minutes ago you told me I deserved it!"

The accusation brought the life back into his face. Instantly the marauding shark was buried beneath a softened, contrite expression.

"A few minutes ago I was out of my head with anger. I didn't mean—"

"Yes, you did," she snapped. "And so did he. He was angry, too. Furiously angry. And he'd been drinking—a bad combination."

He moved his fingers soothingly once again over her bare throat and shoulders, and she felt herself quieting beneath his touch. "Don't be upset, honey. We'll talk about it some other time."

"The subject is closed," she flung back grimly. "I should never have let you open it."

"You didn't have much choice," he murmured blandly, his fingertips still making those slow, lazy, soothing motions on her shoulders as she sat clutching the silk dress.

There was a silence between them as Kendra recovered herself, and Case watched her with gentle speculation. She knew he was wondering about what had happened two years ago, knew he was curious about her current behavior.

"Did you start the self-defense training as a way of rebuilding your self-confidence?" he finally hazarded with keen perception.

"I've told you I don't want to talk about it. Any of it," she said wearily.

"It had been working, hadn't it?" he went on thoughtfully. "When you walked through the door downstairs tonight I was looking at a woman who wasn't afraid of anything in the world. You'd really convinced yourself that you could handle any man who got out of line. And your success with Phelps must have put the final cap on your confidence. You took him out as if he were a helpless child."

"Please, Case . . ."

"But don't you know that no matter how good you are, there's always someone who's a little tougher, a little more experienced? You may have learned how to take care of yourself, but you didn't learn the common sense to go along with it!"

"I've told you I don't want to talk about it!"

"Okay," he conceded with a sigh, "we'll talk about it later. We have a lot to discuss, you and I."

"Don't be ridiculous. We're never going to see each other again. I just want to go home . . ."

"To San Francisco?" he concluded helpfully.

"And I don't want you having Wolf do any more checking up on me!"

He smiled slowly. "We'll talk about everything in the morning," he pacified, his hand on her chin moving to tangle itself briefly in her long, tousled hair. He withdrew it at once when she flinched.

"Kendra, there's nothing to worry about. I won't hurt you. Can't you believe in me, trust me that much? If I'd been going to do something violent, it would have been a few minutes ago in the heat of anger."

She shivered, nodding. "Yes."

"And I was angry," he added dryly.

"I know."

"So for two years you haven't had any sort of normal relationship? Never fallen in love?"

"No!"

"But you've gotten yourself back to the point where you don't mind a few kisses, caresses?" he persisted.

"That's all I want from a relationship now, Case. As I said, even if I hadn't tried to get out of here, you would have found me a—a cheat." She focused on the potted palm across the room. Such a lovely fantasy room. But reality had intruded very heavily, destroying all the warm illusion.

"I don't think I would have felt cheated," he countered softly.

She snapped her head around, alarmed anew at the deepening note in his voice.

"Relax. You have my word that I won't push you beyond your own limits."

"Case, no, I don't want—"

But he was tugging her tenderly against his bare chest, letting her hold the dress in clenched fists between them. She wanted to protest, wanted to beg him not to touch her again, but the words wouldn't come. She was exhausted, physically and mentally and emotionally.

He dropped a velvety warm kiss on her brow, using one hand to push a lock of hair back over her shoulder. Then his lips moved with fine sensitivity to her temples, her ears.

Kendra felt her inner shiver breaking through the rigidity of her body.

"You admitted you were enjoying some aspects of what happened between us," he whispered persuasively. "All I'm asking now is that you let yourself enjoy them again. . . ."

"Not after what's happened! It's not possible!" she cried, turning her face into the hair-sprinkled skin of his shoulder as his arms went gently around her.

"*Especially* after what's happened," he contradicted firmly. "Do you think I want you going home in the morning able to remember only that I nearly raped you? God, Kendra! Let me erase some of those memories I just gave you!"

"No," she protested against his skin, already aware of the warm, male scent of him. "You'll want more than I can give. Men always want more!"

"I'm not denying that," he agreed with a low, rueful groan. "But I won't take any more. You have my word. Just let me hold you for a while, touch you, feel your body next to mine . . ."

His voice held that gentle, coaxing, soothing note again, the one her buried senses had responded to when he'd called them out of hiding. Strong but tender hands moved along the length of her back from the nape of her neck to her waist, gliding under the fall of her hair.

"There is passion in you, Kendra Loring. You seduced me until I couldn't think of anything except getting you into bed, and then you turned into a tigress before my eyes! You set a man's head spinning, do you know that?"

He was lowering himself backward onto the carpet, pulling her down on top of him. There was no painful urgency in his hold, only a light pressure that brought her onto his chest, still gripping the dress.

Kendra's hair fanned out across his naked body, and his gaze flared as he felt the silky touch.

"I wanted to take your hair down during dinner," he confessed with a small, very male grin. He plunged his hands into it. "I was wracking my brain, while you ate the duckling and drank my wine, trying to think of a way to talk you into staying the night."

"I certainly never intended to do any such thing. I would never have come back here with you if you hadn't threatened to make things difficult at the hotel. Oh, Case! None of this should ever have happened! If you hadn't forced me to return this evening, I could have left in the morning with nothing changed!" she wailed helplessly.

"I know you're going to hate me for saying this," he growled, "but I may have done you a hell of a favor this evening!"

"You mean restraining yourself from raping me?" she said bitterly. "Thanks!"

"I meant by having taken you down a peg or two before you got yourself in really hot water, you little idiot," he retorted, his hands sliding onto her shoulders and kneading them sensually. "I know this isn't a good time to ask you to see reason—"

"Reason!"

"But try and imagine how you'd be feeling now if you had tried your tricks on someone else who'd had as much back-alley experience as I've had but who didn't bother to curb his desire for revenge!"

He was right. Knowing he was right only made things worse somehow.

"Honey, you're an amateur. Your technique is good, but you lack real-life experience."

"I seem to be getting that tonight!"

His mouth twisted in acknowledgment of her heavy

sarcasm. "You remind me of the guy who takes a few karate lessons and then starts wandering down tough streets with hundred-dollar bills hanging out of his pockets! No common sense. You bought yourself a feeling of power and didn't bother to consider the fact that there are other folks out here in the world with just as much of it and more. And in the last analysis you panicked."

She dropped her face into her hands, which were resting on his chest. That accusation was probably the worst of all.

Again his fingers moved caressingly, soothingly over her skin. "The real world isn't a safe practice mat, sweetheart. It's good to know how to protect yourself, but the best defense is to stay clear of trouble, not to welcome it with open arms!"

"I didn't!" She lifted hurt, offended eyes up to his face. "What should I have done? How should I have gotten out of here tonight? I tried to talk my way out! You wouldn't let me go!"

"You weren't in any danger, and I think you knew that," he countered, his mouth tightening. "I would have let you sleep alone tonight if that's really what you would have wanted."

"That's not what was worrying me! I wanted to stay clear of you, don't you understand? I should never even have agreed to have dinner in the first place. Now you already know too much. . . ."

"Hush," he breathed, stopping her lips with a finger. "Hush, Kendra. No more talking. Just calm down, relax."

She wanted to argue, go on accusing him, anything to keep him from using his hands on her like this. But it was rapidly becoming impossible. Before, when she had been under attack, she had found a refuge for her assaulted senses deep in her mind by using an aspect of her training. It was a method of focusing one's inner will, and it had worked then.

Now her senses no longer responded to her attempts to withdraw them. They were luxuriating in Case's gentle touch, beginning to rediscover greedily the beguiling masculinity slowly enveloping them. She knew that in spite of her deliberate reasoning to the contrary, she trusted Case Garrett. If he had wanted to hurt her, he would have done it already under the extreme provocation she'd provided.

Earlier she had been intent on escape. Now she was still too stunned to think of anything except the moment. In that weakened state Case's sensitive, erotic touch was unbelievably seductive. She found herself longing to surrender to it and forget everything else, past and future.

"I'm glad you like this part of making love at least," he whispered wistfully. "Because even when you were trying to murder me, all I wanted to do was kiss you and go on kissing you—"

"I wasn't trying to murder you!"

He laughed affectionately, pulling her surreptitiously a little closer and shifting her onto her side. Bracing himself on one elbow, he trailed a warm hand along the curve of her waist and hip, and then lowered his head.

She didn't pull away from the kiss, nor did she try to remain passive beneath the slow, inviting touch of his mouth. She simply, completely, incredibly, gave herself up to the embrace with a long, tremulous sigh.

The resistance went out of her, pushed aside by the wonder of Case's hands and lips. She would worry about the morning when it came. For the first time in two years she stopped thinking of the past and the future and of protecting herself both physically and emotionally. She wanted only to let the sensations ripple across her nerves, reawakening them, arousing them, comforting them.

Case murmured Kendra's name thickly against her mouth, and then his tongue was moving hotly, passionately but with infinite control. He urged her response and after a moment it came. There ensued a fascinating little duel carried out in the secret cavern of her mouth, and all the while his hands continued to caress and excite.

"Oh . . . !"

Kendra twisted, dropping the tattered silk dress and spreading her hands across his chest instead. She heard him groan as her nails softly discovered the path of his black, curling chest hair, which tapered toward his lean waist.

"You go to my head," he said, withdrawing reluctantly from her mouth and seeking the delicate tip of her ear. She felt his teeth sink into the skin with delicate finesse. It sent tremors throughout her whole body, and she knew he felt them.

But the shivers weren't from fear this time, and she explored the pleasure they brought with growing exhilaration. Something exquisite and primitive uncurled in the region of her stomach, and her leg moved, seeking the hard roughness of his thigh.

"That's it, little kitten, come close. I'll take care of you. You won't lack for anything." His hand smoothed over her hip, curving around one resilient buttock.

Her fingertips clenched into the thrusting muscles of his back as her body arched toward him, and once more she moaned, this time with undisguised desire.

She felt him trace exciting patterns down to the inside of her thigh, using his leg to open her to him. She gasped when he finally touched the heart of her rising passion, her breath catching deep in her throat.

Kendra opened her eyes very wide and assimilated the lambent fire in him, knowing it was beginning to rage again but was still safely in check. If she asked him to stop now, she knew he would.

"Let me make love to you tonight," he pleaded, touching the tip of his tongue to the pulse at the base of her throat. "Please give yourself to me. I want you so badly!"

"Oh, Case, I can't seem to think. . . ."

"You don't need to think. I've done all the thinking for both of us. Trust me, sweetheart. Put yourself in my care. You want me, I can tell. I can feel the soft warmth in you waiting for me."

She trembled again as he moved his hand erotically, sensuously at the juncture of her thighs, and she let him push her back into the thick white carpet. She had the momentary image of lying on white fur, and then he was coming down slowly on top of her, and she was reaching up to pull him close.

"Kendra!"

He rasped her name against her shoulder as he rained hot kisses down toward her breasts. She felt her nipples tauten into hard peaks as he circled the dark pink area around them with his fingers, and she lifted herself against his hand.

His lips and tongue came down to replace his fingers, and a light-headed feeling swept her, dizzying and dazzling as she uttered his name and a plea.

"Case! Case! Please . . . !"

"Shall we be lovers tonight, sweetheart? Will you let me give you what I'm longing to give? Take what I need?"

"Yes, oh, yes, please!"

Her eyes shut against the unexpected impact of pulsing desire, Kendra clamped her fingers into his hair as he moved slowly, gracefully, masterfully against her. She lifted her hips, curving herself around him, taking him into her with a possessiveness that would astound her later.

"Ah . . . !"

She gloried as the passion finally broke free in him, plunging beyond control and pulling them both into the maelstrom they had created. Her nails raked through his hair, dislodging the velvet eyepatch and sending it flying onto the carpet. In that moment neither noticed.

Then she was clinging to his strength, giving herself up to the wild rhythm, wanting only to please and be pleased. She didn't ask herself how this tender, engulfing passion could have ensued from the savage battle earlier. She didn't ask herself how a man who could threaten to kill another man, who could make his living in the shadowy world of gambling, who could virtually kidnap her, could also become a man full of restraint, finesse, and fiercely gentle passion while having sex.

Those questions would come later. For now there was only the sensation of overpowering need, the feel of the thick carpet beneath her, the erotic weight of this man making love to her, and the driving desire. They combined to swamp her senses. She felt the wild, uncurling response as it struck through her body, and she cried out the name of the man creating it.

It seemed to galvanize him into a last, exultant display of strength, tenderness, and power. Case gripped Kendra so tightly, his fingers digging urgently into the skin of her shoulders, she felt as if they were one being, and then she lost her breath for an instant. A violent convulsion shook her, sending her into a shivering reaction of pleasure such as she had never known.

Her thick, impeded shout was lost in his mouth as he drained the shimmering energy from her and filled her with his own.

Slowly, as if she were floating, Kendra came out of the intense, pleasure-filled world Case had shown her. She became aware of a warm, slightly rough palm moving over the curve of her stomach and thighs like a cat's tongue. A voice, Case's voice, spoke in her ear with the beguiling touch of a magician.

"Sleep, my mystery lady. Don't try to come out of the fog tonight. Just go to sleep. The talking can come in the morning. . ."

The temptation to obey the spell-creating voice was too much. Kendra sighed deeply, never opening her eyes. She felt herself lifted and placed onto the bed; felt his warm, damp body coming down beside her, and then she was asleep.

CHAPTER SIX

Kendra turned the key in the door of her Victorian town house with an incredible sense of relief. For the first time in hours she managed to shake off the sensation of pursuit.

It was a ridiculous feeling, having no basis in reality. She had, after all, been safe since she had boarded her flight back from Lake Tahoe. Besides, there was no reason to think Case Garrett would have any particular desire to follow her. He'd gotten what he'd wanted. In his world, such brief encounters were commonplace. She had represented an amusing interlude that had temporarily intrigued him.

The litany was the same one that had been going through her head since she'd awakened that morning in the huge white bed and found him asleep on the pillow beside her. The black velvet of his lashes replaced the missing eyepatch, concealing the empty ruin of his left eye. The darkness of his thick, tousled hair against the white pillow had been almost heart-wrenchingly attractive to her.

He lay with the crisp whiteness of the sheet pulled only to his waist, and the bronzed skin of his chest and shoulders made her wonder how a gambler, a man of the night, ever got such a natural tan. Sunlamps, probably, she'd told herself with sudden disgust.

Without allowing herself further thought, she'd slipped from the bed, forcing her mind to concentrate on nothing but escape. He stirred briefly as she slid, naked, off the bed, but he didn't awaken.

Kendra wasted no time. Grabbing her suitcase, she'd hurried into the tropical living room. She'd pulled on her tweed skirt, copper-colored blouse, and her blazer. Snatching up her purse and coat, she'd let herself out the door, suitcase in one hand.

Unlike the other, larger casinos, Garrett's was not open twenty-four hours a day. In the light of dawn she found it empty. The felt-covered tables stood silent, and the roulette wheel looked like a toy instead of the dangerous menace it could become. Wolf had been nowhere in sight.

She'd found a cab to the airport, caught an earlier flight than she'd originally scheduled, and had landed in San Francisco in the rain.

Never had the lush, yellow-gold and white interior of her home looked so welcoming. Kendra shut the door behind her and crossed the Oriental rug, which created an effective foil for the almost-French-style furnishings of the living room.

A great deal of her profits from the employment agency in which she was a partner had gone into creating the luxurious, romantic surroundings. Twin banquettes, their white covers edged in gold fringe, framed the sweeping bay window. Gold pillows were artfully strewn on each. An ornate gilt mirror and a lacquered Queen Anne secretary added opulence to the room. French-style chairs and an elegant inlaid tea table provided another sumptuous touch.

The French theme spilled over into the dining room, with its oval table beneath a small, delicate crystal chandelier. The bedroom had been done to create a charming study in addition to a sleeping area. A graceful lacquered desk and several bookcases occupied a portion of the room. Another large Oriental carpet extended from the sitting area into the section occupied by the wide, low bed. Across the bed was a rich fur throw.

As with her clothes, Kendra indulged herself in her home. She made no apology for either. It pleased her, and she had no one else in the world to worry about pleasing except herself.

The phone rang an hour later as she emerged from a hot, reviving shower.

"You're back! Thank God! Tell me what happened, Kendra. Did he accept the check? Did he say anything about—about me?" Her cousin's anxious voice came over the line, conveying a picture of the delicate, small-boned creature on the other end.

At twenty-six, Donna Radburn was a beautiful woman. Small, graceful, with a lovely profile, she was blessed with luminous green eyes, jet-black hair, which fell in a heavy curve to her shoulders, and a creamy complexion. She had an instinctive way of handling men that Kendra, in her younger years, would have dearly loved to imitate. There was a helpless, feminine quality about Donna that seemed to draw forth the protective instincts in most men. For a while it had seemed as if Austin Radburn had succumbed to the spell, too.

"He took the check, Donna," Kendra said calmly, making up her mind that she would never tell Donna what had happened the previous night between herself and Case Garrett. But there were other things Donna should know. "There was a problem, though . . ."

"What happened, Kendra?"

"Someone followed me. He was sent by Austin to ask me questions about you."

"Oh, God!"

"I know. He didn't get any answers, of course, but we have to face the fact that Austin's aware that you might have contacted me. I think we'd better not meet too often

95

until things are settled, and you'd probably better not come over here—"

"Kendra, I'll go crazy if I can't talk to someone. Jason's already driving me out of my mind! If I don't have another adult—"

"Calm down, Donna," Kendra soothed, thinking that she sounded, ironically, a bit like Case had sounded last night. "It's okay. We'll get out and do things so you won't get cabin fever. I'm just saying that we probably ought to be careful about you being over here. If Austin really thinks I know where you are, he's liable to hire someone else to watch the place or something."

"You're right. I know you're right. I'll be so thankful when the divorce is final and I have that money. . . ."

Kendra drew a deep breath before saying very carefully, "Have you thought about what's going to happen when you do have the money, Donna?"

"What do you mean?"

"I mean, the divorce being final might not stop Austin."

"With the money Dad left, I can afford to move Jason and myself halfway around the world. I can get lost until Austin gives up!" Donna declared firmly.

Kendra wasn't so sure, but there was no doubt that her cousin knew Austin a great deal better than Kendra did. Perhaps Donna was right in her analysis. Perhaps Austin would eventually give up, especially after he knew Donna had her hands on the money.

"Kendra, about Case Garrett . . ." Donna began hesitantly.

"What about him?" Kendra asked stonily, not wanting to converse at all on that particular subject.

"Did he . . . ask about me? Did he ask about the rest of the money?"

Kendra heard the worried note in Donna's voice and again tried to calm her. "I told him he'd have the rest of it in a couple of months. He seemed to accept that."

"I can't thank you enough for handling this for me. I was so embarrassed . . ."

"I don't see why. He wasn't angry or threatening about the money," Kendra observed with an effort to be honest about the matter. "I think he would have taken it from you without a fuss."

"You don't understand," Donna sighed. "Things were so bad during the time I ran up that debt. I was feeling so terrible, so depressed. I did things I can't even believe now—"

"There's no point in talking about it again, Donna," Kendra murmured, thinking of how bad Donna had really been. Her violent depression, her drinking, her gambling, and her attempted suicide seemed incredible to contemplate now.

"I know. I just want to tell you how much I appreciate your facing him. I couldn't have done it—not after the way I behaved the last time I saw him!"

Kendra frowned, wondering exactly what had happened, but she sensed Donna wasn't in a mood to go into detail, and Kendra wasn't sure she wanted to hear those details. Donna had been at a very low point in her life, reckless and wild and scared. Case Garrett was a man who knew how to soothe frightened women. No, Kendra didn't want to think about what might have happened between her beautiful cousin and Case Garrett.

"Listen, according to the weather report, it's supposed to clear up this afternoon," Kendra said encouragingly, wanting to change the subject. "Why don't you take Jason out to Golden Gate Park? I'll meet you at the Japanese Tea Garden, and we can take him to the aquarium. He'll love that."

"Do you think it's safe?"

"I think so. The important thing is that you probably shouldn't risk coming here. It will take Austin a while to find someone else to keep an eye on me, if he decides to pursue that route. I'll be careful going out to the park. If I don't show up by, say, two o'clock, assume I decided there was somebody following and turned back, okay?"

"I'd really like to get out," Donna admitted. "As I said, Jason is driving me up the walls."

"Just a normal five-year-old. He needs some outdoor exercise."

"Why is it that the nonmothers of this world are always such experts on children!" Donna managed a small laugh.

"It's easy. When you know you can walk away from a kid at any time and leave the problems to someone else, there's no trick to being objective!"

By the time Kendra reached the lovely formal tea garden, Jason, a lively picture with his cap of shining black hair and his mother's green eyes, had already fed his entire lunch to the squirrels. He'd gone on to nearly throttle a duck, climb over every miniature bridge in the magnificent five acres, and barely avoid drowning in the numerous reflective pools.

Donna looked up in heartfelt relief when Kendra appeared, walking down one of the tiny paths toward the bench beside the pagoda where the younger woman sat.

"You made it! I was beginning to worry."

"Hi, Kendra!" Jason paused momentarily to call out before racing back over another miniature bridge. The serene beauty of the garden was lost on him, Kendra decided affectionately, but he took his own brand of pleasure out of the experience.

"Hi, Jason!" she smiled warmly. Once there had been a time when she had thought having a family would be one of her goals in life. She had missed badly the loving interaction she had experienced with her own parents, and a part of her wanted to recreate it with a new generation. Those thoughts had gone underground two years ago, only to resurface recently when little Jason had come back into her life. She wondered idly if Case Garrett had ever thought of having a family. But families didn't exactly go with his current life-style, she decided wryly.

"There was no problem," she remarked to Donna. "I just took a few precautions, like wandering around through the park for a while before coming here to the garden. I'm sure no one followed me. I don't even think it would have been possible, considering the traffic today!"

Donna smiled in shaky relief. "I know I'm nervous. I wish it were over!"

"It will be soon," Kendra told her forcefully. "What do you say we get Jason before he attempts to climb the Buddha and take him to the aquarium?"

"Good idea!"

They spent the afternoon awing Jason with the strange and magnificent creatures of the deep housed in the large Steinhart Aquarium, exhausting themselves in a futile attempt to tire Jason. At the end of the day Kendra saw them off in a cab and located her own sleek little sports car in the parking lot. When she found herself glancing continually in the mirror she lectured herself on trying not to be paranoid. No one could have followed her through Sunday traffic. But she also knew something of Austin Radburn. . . .

On Monday afternoon she was deep into a folder of résumés from marketing managers, searching for the perfect candidate to present to an important client, when her partner in the agency, Norris Webb, knocked on her door.

She glanced up and smiled at the man who stood in her office doorway. Norris was thirty-nine years old, a tawny-haired man whose smiling brown eyes, polished appearance, and easygoing charm had made him an instant success in the employment business. He was an attractive man, presently divorced, and Kendra knew he didn't lack for feminine companionship. He was also making the same healthy profit out of the business as was she.

"Just wanted to remind you we have that dinner meeting with the Richardson clients." He grinned. His hand rested lightly on one hip, thrusting back the gray pinstriped jacket of his three-piece suit. Like Kendra, he was every inch the well-dressed San Francisco executive.

"I haven't forgotten. It's your turn to pick me up, though."

"I'll be there with bells on. Seven o'clock all right?"

"That will be fine. Did you want to take them to that little Italian place in North Beach?"

"Nothing but the best for these folks! If we get their account, we'll be sitting very pretty for the next year and a half!"

"We'll get it," she assured him and watched him smile and walk off. Thoughtfully she leaned back in the huge swivel chair, idly smoothing the black wool skirt of her suit.

She and Norris had been in business together for over five years. For the first two and a half years of that partnership, he had been married. Norris had been very much in love with his beautiful young wife, and the divorce had shaken him. By the time he had begun looking around for new female acquaintances, however, his relationship with Kendra had become so firmly established as a business association that he hadn't even attempted to transform it into something else. Kendra had been happy enough to keep her business life separated from her social one.

Then there had been the awful night two years ago. After that Kendra had kept her social life nearly as cool as her professional one. She had stopped seeing men who pressured her for more than casual relationships, restricting her dating to those who were content with a sophisticated evening out and who demanded nothing more than a kiss at the door or over after-theater brandy. The business evenings with Norris Webb fit nicely into that life-style.

The evening entertaining the Richardson Electronics people went well. The food was superb at the tiny, extravagant Italian restaurant in the Bohemian quarter of the city, and the tab picked up by the Loring-Webb agency reflected it. But the results were worth it, as Kendra told Norris on the way back to her flat.

"They'll be signing the papers in the morning." She smiled in satisfaction. "We'll have to get busy collecting the kind of résumés they'll need during the next few months."

"We've already got a lot of good ones on file. I think we'd better concentrate on filling that comptroller position first, though. They seem most concerned about that."

Kendra nodded as Norris slid his white Mercedes into a parking slot in front of her home, turning his wheels into the curb of the steep hill as every San Franciscan did by second nature.

He assisted her out of the car with automatic gallantry, smiling as she turned up the collar of her coat and dug the key out of her silver purse.

"Want to come in for a nightcap?" she invited, smiling up at him pleasantly. It was nothing unusual. He often did after a business evening such as this.

"Sounds good. I see your neighbor is still up. A bit late for her, isn't it?" Norris nodded toward the lights in the downstairs flat.

"Mrs. Colter is probably watching another old Bogart movie. She loves them!"

"It's a good night for it." Norris grinned. "All this cold, damp fog. San Francisco could have been used to film that sort of movie."

As if to punctuate his statement, a distant foghorn sounded forlornly, warning ships on the bay. Kendra shivered uneasily and wondered at her own imagination. Fog shrouded the streetlamps, lending a sense of impending doom to the quiet street scene. It made her think of dark subjects like old Bogart films and men who made their livings in a night world of danger and sophisticated menace. Men, for example, who ran gambling casinos.

Deliberately Kendra forced herself to find something matter-of-fact to discuss as she opened the front security door, led the way past Mrs. Colter's entrance, and started up the stairs to her own flat.

"You know, I've been thinking about the comptroller position. Have you seen the Caldwell résumé? I talked to her last week, and I think she might be an excellent possibility. She's—"

Kendra broke off her words as the door to Mrs. Colter's flat opened and the spry, gray-haired lady stuck her head around the corner to greet her upstairs neighbor.

"There you are, Kendra. About time you got back. Hello, Mr. Webb," she added cheerfully, nodding to the familiar man on the step below Kendra. "Have a good evening?"

"Excellent," Norris confirmed, one tawny brow lifting in polite inquiry. It was not like Mrs. Colter to question him when he brought Kendra home. "And yourself?"

"A very interesting evening, young man," the elderly lady declared in tones of deepest satisfaction. "One you'll be amused to hear about, Kendra," she added.

"A good film, Mrs. Colter?" Kendra smiled indulgently, pausing with one hand on the railing to glance back.

"Better than a film, my dear. Real life sometimes is, although not often. I've been entertaining a visitor for you while you were out."

Kendra took one look at Mrs. Colter's snapping blue eyes and her fingers clutched the railing. Radburn. Had Austin Radburn himself come after her?

For a split second the panic welled up inside—the panic she hadn't expected to feel if she ever met him again but which had been unleashed by the events of her evening in Lake Tahoe. She would never again feel the cool, confident sense of safety she had cultivated for the past two years. It had been wiped out by Case Garrett.

But she was not alone tonight. She had Norris with her. Surely another man . . .

"Good evening, Kendra."

Kendra's eyes flew to meet the shockingly familiar dark gaze of the black-haired man standing behind a smiling Mrs. Colter. The black velvet patch was in place as usual, and Case was wearing an obviously hand-tailored suit of near-black wool. He looked coolly, darkly powerful, and she was struck with an awful feeling of inevitability.

Summoning her startled senses, Kendra nodded toward him. "Hello, Case. What are you doing here?"

"I came to see you, of course. Aren't you going to introduce me to your friend?"

Norris looked blankly from one to the other, a trace of awkwardness in his smile.

"A friend of yours?" he asked his partner.

"Norris, this is Case Garrett. Norris Webb."

The two men regarded each other, Case inclining his head almost regally in acknowledgment of the introduction but not extending a hand. It was left for Norris to initiate that small action.

"Look, Kendra, we can talk another time. I'll be seeing you in the office tomorrow . . ." Norris began a bit hastily as Mrs. Colter stepped back to allow Case to walk past her and out into the hall.

"There's no need to rush off, Norris," she began, knowing it was a losing battle.

"I'm sure Mr. Webb has no wish to be in the way," Case was saying smoothly, coming up the stairs to put a proprietary arm around her waist and effectively shouldering Norris aside.

"No, of course not," Norris agreed quickly. "I'll be on

my way. See you tomorrow, Kendra. Good night, Mrs. Colter."

"Good night," Mrs. Colter called brightly as the three of them watched Norris Webb let himself out the door. The older woman turned back to eye Kendra interestedly. "Good thing I was home, isn't it? Otherwise Case might have had to wait out in the cold!"

"Thank you, Mrs. Colter." Kendra sighed feebly, turning to climb the rest of the stairs with a quick, brittle stride.

Case echoed her thanks to Mrs. Colter, and then he was walking into the flat behind Kendra, his eye roving appreciatively around the opulently romantic room.

"So this is where you fled with such haste yesterday morning! Very nice. It looks like you: very tasteful but very first-class!"

Kendra didn't reply to that. She discovered her fingers were shaking as she undid the buttons of her coat. Instantly he was behind her, removing it with well-timed courtesy. She felt his touch on her shoulders and stepped quickly away, turning to face him as he stood holding her red wool coat. She was wearing a winter white knit dress that hugged her slenderness, the long sleeves and high neck an enchanting contrast to the sensuous fit of the knee-length dress.

"All right, Case. What's this all about? Why have you come here?"

"Who is he, Kendra?" he demanded softly, ignoring her question. His gaze bored into her, seeking answers to a query he had no right to make.

"Norris Webb is my partner. We own an employment agency. And besides, it's none of your business, Case. Why are you here?" She faced him, her chin held high, her neatly knotted hair sleek in the soft hall light. She knew she must have appeared defiant, but she couldn't help it. It was how she felt: defiant and resentful and angry.

"Are you thinking of making him your lover?" Case bit out softly, walking toward her and tossing the red coat down on one of the yellow-gold upholstered French chairs. He moved past her into the living room, not touching her. She turned and watched helplessly as he prowled through the room, examining the elaborate gilt frame of the mirror, the crystal vase sitting on the lacquered secretary, and the Japanese flower arrangement on the tea table. Then he glanced up broodingly.

"I didn't unwrap my mystery present only to hand it over to another man, Kendra."

Kendra felt the blood drain from her cheeks. "Why, you incredible egotist!" she breathed.

"Why did you leave yesterday without saying goodbye?" he asked almost conversationally as he settled down onto one of the white-and-gold banquettes in front of the bay window. He leaned lazily into the corner, one arm resting along the back of the banquette, and looked at her with a directness that scared Kendra.

"I should think the answer is obvious," she said in a low voice, walking slowly over to the opposite banquette and sinking down into it without meeting his gaze. Her knees felt weak with the unexpected shock of his appearance. How could he do this to her? What did he want? "What happened between us was a mistake I would very much like to forget!"

"No!" he denied in a deep growl.

She stared at him, her resentment plain in the narrowed hazel eyes. "Tell yourself anything you want to hear, Case. I don't much care. If you want to take the credit for discovering my secret, then go ahead. If your ego likes the idea of having 'reawakened' me, then tell yourself that. But I would very much appreciate it if you would leave me alone."

"Kendra, what the hell is wrong?" he rasped, sitting up to eye her intently, his elbows resting on his knees. "Why are you acting like this? When you went to sleep in my arms the other night, you were all soft and trusting, and now you look at me as if I were some kind of monster!"

Her mouth twisted wryly but she said nothing.

"Why did you leave like that?" he asked again, the honesty of his question gravelling his voice. "I'd told you that you could go in the morning. I wasn't going to force you to stay!"

"I just wanted to get away, can't you understand? How did I know what you were going to do next?" she retorted wretchedly.

"You didn't trust me? I don't believe that!"

"Then believe what you damn well want to believe!"

"Kendra!"

"Please leave me alone, Case!"

"No, dammit! You left behind as many questions as you answered that night. I want to know everything, honey. Everything!"

"You don't have that right," she whispered flatly.

"The hell I don't! You gave me that right when you gave yourself to me. What is it, Kendra? Were you frightened of the commitment, after all? Were you afraid to face the fact that you're still a woman? Were you shocked to find out your passions run so deep after all this time? Tell me what drove you away without even saying good-bye!"

She glared at him in seething silence, wondering how he could be so insensitive. Didn't he even have an inkling as to what he'd done to her? No, like any man, the only thing he could relate to was the lovemaking. She gritted her teeth.

"I'd rather not discuss this, Case. Can't you understand that? After what you did to me—"

"What I did to you!" he repeated, looking suddenly appalled. "After what I *did* to you! Kendra! Are you going to sit there and accuse me of rape? My God, woman, it was no such thing!"

106

She surged to her feet, fists clenched at her sides. "No, I don't imagine you'd see it that way!"

"Because it wasn't that way!" He was on his feet now, too, frustrated anger evident in every line of his lean, hard body.

Unwillingly Kendra remembered the feel of that body against hers and turned away from him, focusing blindly on the mirror across from her.

He put out a hand, grasping her shoulder and spinning her around to face him. "Tell me the truth! Do you really think that what happened between us was rape? Tell me, Kendra!"

"All you can think about is the sex, isn't it, Case? That's all your male ego wants to remember. But something else happened to me that night. Something for which I might not be reasonably able to blame you but which I can never forget. Don't you understand?" she concluded on a desperate plea. "Don't you understand what you did to me when you threw me to the floor and held me there until I realized there was nothing I could do to defend myself?"

He stared at her, the first glimmer of comprehension evident in the narrowed gaze and tightened mouth.

"Oh, my God, Kendra!" he muttered hoarsely. "Don't hold that against me! You *can't* !"

"I agree," she shot back tightly. "Logically I can't. I attacked and you countered. You had every right. But when you did you tore apart something I've been building for two solid years. You destroyed the self-confidence I've worked so hard to give myself in place of the fear I'd been living with. You showed me how weak I really am. Don't expect me to thank you for that, Case Garrett!"

"Dammit, Kendra! What else could I have done? Sooner or later you would have gotten yourself into serious trouble! You were overly confident, inviting disaster. You were lucky with Phelps, but it could so easily have gone against you! Kendra, even with me, you almost went too far. The last thing in the world I wanted to do was hurt you, but I very nearly did. God, but you were arrogant! You could have been challenging a man who wouldn't have cared how badly he treated you in retaliation, and then where would you have been? Beaten *and* raped!"

Kendra took a grip on herself, wondering at the desperation in him. Why did it matter so much to him? His ego, she supposed sadly.

"I know you think I should remember only that you got me to surrender willingly, but that's not the way I'll recall that night, Case," she told him evenly. "For me that memory will always be mixed up with the casual destruction of the wall against fear I spent two years building. Every time I think of you, I will remember that you were the one who showed me I had only created an illusion for myself. Do you honestly expect me to forget what you did to me?"

CHAPTER SEVEN

If Kendra's common sense hadn't denied it, she would have sworn that the emotion that flickered in Case's right eye was one of pain. Whatever it was, it disappeared beneath the exasperated irritation that gripped him. He gave her a small shake.

"Apparently the memory of what happened between us isn't completely obliterated by the fact that I didn't let you clobber me!" he snapped. "You obviously had plans to continue reestablishing normal relationships with men!"

"What are you talking about?" She gritted, angry at his typically masculine approach to the issue. He was incapable of understanding exactly what he'd done to her.

"I'm talking about Norris Webb, dammit! You were leading him up your stairs tonight, remember? Anxious to show him how you've blossomed lately?"

"What a disgusting thing to say! Norris has often come in with me after an evening out! We're business partners, not lovers, although I don't see what difference it should make to you!" she blazed.

His fingers dug into the nubby fabric of her dress, and she saw the taut lines of tension around his mouth. "It makes a great deal of difference. You and I *are* lovers, and I know it probably sounds outdated, but I have no intention of sharing you with your business partner!"

"For your information," she mocked furiously, "one night in bed does not make us lovers!"

"How about two nights?"

Before she fully realized his intention Kendra was in his arms. Hard and sinewy with the warm strength she remembered so well, his embrace swept her close against the roughened texture of his suit jacket. She inhaled the faint spicy tang of an expensive after-shave mixed with the clean, male scent of him, and the tantalizing combination made her quiver.

"Case, stop it, please!"

"No," he denied huskily, his deep voice sinking to a low, caressing level that stimulated her nerve endings. "I came down to San Francisco to talk to you, but since rational conversation is clearly out of the question, I'll try another method of communication!"

"Why, you conceited, overbearing gang—*gambler*!" Kendra ripped out as he lowered his head to her mouth. She stumbled over the last word and changed it, but his grip tightened in warning.

His lips closed on hers before she could whip up any more accusations. The kiss was not like the gentle, coaxing caresses she had known in Lake Tahoe. This time he meant to bring her to heel in the quickest possible way.

She made an attempt at struggling, knowing in advance that it would be useless, as indeed it was. He only held her more securely, one arm wrapped around her, pinning her arms to her side. With his other hand he gently but firmly fixed her head in place. As his mouth moved hungrily, heavily on hers the memories of the night in Lake Tahoe flooded back, driving out her fierce resentment.

"I know you don't think I'm good enough for you; that you've automatically classified me as some sort of lowlife because of the way I make my living," he rasped harshly against her mouth. "And now you resent me because I made you face reality. But none of that is going to keep you from melting in my arms again the way you did the other night!"

110

"No, dammit, I won't—"

The rest of her words were muffled as he took advantage of her parted lips to probe the heated honey of her mouth. His tongue assaulted with seductive menace, tangling with hers until she moaned and trembled in his grasp.

"Did you really believe I'd let you walk away from me so easily?"

"What do you want from me?" It was a plea. Kendra's lashes were tightly shut against the overpowering pleasure of his touch, as if by not looking at him she could pretend he didn't exist.

"A great many things, Kendra Loring. A great many things."

She felt her feet leave the floor, and her mind whirled with momentary dizziness as he lifted her into his arms. Her eyes flew open as she clutched instinctively at his neck.

"This won't make any difference, Case. I'm not going to get involved in an affair with you!"

"You already are," he murmured simply, starting down the short hall.

There was no trick to finding her bedroom in the one-bedroom apartment, and Kendra felt a kind of helpless rage as he used his foot to open the door to the darkened room.

"You really do like the finer things, don't you?" he growled in amusement as he settled her lightly on the bed and moved his hands deeply into the thick fur throw on which she lay. "But don't worry, honey, I can afford them."

"How dare you!" she said in soft outrage, pulling herself into a sitting position as he stripped off his jacket.

"If I weren't a little reckless at times, I probably wouldn't be where I am tonight," he retorted, his mocking grin a slash of menace in the dim light.

She tried to move, sliding across the heavy fur, but he

was much faster. Case sat beside her, clasping her ankle in one hand while he eased off his shoes before she could get more than a few inches away.

"Case, if you have any consideration for me at all—"

"Oh, I do!" he vowed humorously, his fingers going to the buttons of his shirt.

"Then kindly remember that I haven't been seeing anyone seriously in two years!" she snapped. "Other than the other night I haven't—haven't been with anyone. I'm not *prepared,* for God's sake!"

"Do you think I haven't thought of that?" he soothed gently. "In fact, there's a possibility that you're already pregnant, isn't there?"

Kendra swallowed heavily, throwing one arm over her eyes in despair. The idea of again going through that trauma of waiting and hoping that she wasn't pregnant sent a cold shudder through her. She had been deliberately repressing the thought. She'd been lucky two years ago, but what if she . . .

"Hey, honey, it's okay," Case whispered huskily, pulling her protective arm away from her face and gently stroking the side of her cheek as he smiled reassuringly. "What happened the other night is past. Tonight I'll take precautions."

"Thanks," she said bleakly. "And what happens if it's too late?"

"Then," he said calmly, lying down beside her and gathering her into his arms, "I'll take care of you." He eased aside the high collar of the white dress and pressed his lips to her throat.

Kendra was so stunned by his cool words, she couldn't find the courage to ask if he meant by taking care of her that he'd pay for an abortion. She lay very still in his embrace, fighting for the uninterested attitude toward sex that she had felt for the past two years. But Case had

112

demolished that barrier the other night, and tonight he was intent on reminding her of it.

She felt the heat of his body, his naked chest crowding her into the fur. He was wearing only his slacks now, and she felt an irresistible urge to once more find the smooth muscles of his back with her fingers.

"This time you're not going to run away after I've made love to you," he swore as he eased down the zipper of her knit dress, exposing her small, unconfined breasts. "This time we're on your territory, so there's nowhere for you to run!"

"This won't make any difference in my attitude toward you," Kendra flung back as he found her nipple with his lips. She felt the exciting shock waves as he curled his tongue and then his teeth around the tip of her breast, hardening it into a peak of desire.

"You might go on resenting me for a while, but you won't be able to deny yourself or me! I can deal with your resentment as long as I can make you admit you want me!"

"Damn you—" But the cry was blocked in her throat as her skin began to tingle under his caresses. The white dress was pushed down to her hips and then off completely, along with her pantyhose. She was left in only her silky French panties.

"Did you think one night with you was going to be enough for me?" Case growled, his gaze flaming as he swept her body with it. His fingers lazed over her stomach in barely restrained anticipation, and Kendra twisted beneath his touch.

"We shouldn't even have had that!" she whispered huskily as he slipped his hand just inside her panties. His lips were exploring the valley between her breasts, making their way slowly, enticingly down to the region just below her stomach.

"Put your arms around me and say that again," he challenged thickly.

She hesitated and then gave in to the command, knowing already it was what she wanted. She would never be able to deny totally the attraction of this dangerous man. It had been there from the beginning when her eyes had met his gaze across the casino.

The panties were stripped from her, and he scored his nails lightly along the inside of her thigh as she curled against him. When he traced his exquisite patterns ever higher and nearer to the dampening warmth of her, she moaned and sank her teeth into the bronzed skin of his shoulder.

"Did you really think I'd let some other man have all this after I'd made you mine?" he growled as she inflicted the small pain. He retaliated by using his teeth gently on her thigh, sending a fierce wave of urgency through her.

Kendra said nothing. She was beyond speaking coherently now, her mind and her body conspiring to surrender again to the ecstasy she had known once before with this man.

He groaned as she writhed luxuriously against him, and she clenched her hands in his dark hair as he strung kisses along her hip, up to the curve of her waist, into her navel, and finally back to her breasts. All the while his hand never ceased its dazzling play, building her desire to a flaming, demanding height.

"Oh, Case—Case . . ." His name came in little gasps between her lips as she clung to him, her fingers dancing in excitement along his shoulders and down to his still-clothed taut, masculine buttocks. She kneaded the thrusting contours of his body, returning caress for caress as they left the shore and drifted together through the surging current of their mutual desire.

When he rasped her name she took a deep pleasure in

the evidence of his arousal, and her leg shifted on the thick fur with unconscious invitation.

Abruptly he was pulling away from her, whispering softly as he did so.

"Soon, sweetheart, soon. You drive me out of my mind, do you know that?"

She heard him rid himself of his remaining garments, knew he fumbled for a moment longer in the shadows, and then he was back beside her on the fur throw rug, his hands plunging through her hair as he pulled it free of its clip.

He loomed over her, settling his weight along her length, pulling her up into his heat and passion. She went to him willingly, holding him tightly as she experienced the exquisite shock of his claiming.

"Oh, God, Kendra!"

And then there was only the timeless present, the deep and primitive joy of surrendering to a man who understood the true nature of the desire he engendered.

Kendra had told him before that, at its best, sex for a man came into the category of recreation. But she had been wrong, at least about this man. What swept over them both was too powerful, too potent a force to ever be termed *recreation*. It involved an entirely different level of communication, one she hadn't guessed existed before she'd met Case Garrett.

And in the throes of his passion Case couldn't hide the depths of his need. She would have known if the sensation they were living through was affecting him to a lesser degree than it was affecting her. It might be only desire he felt, but it was a shatteringly intense emotion that captured her completely. She could no more have denied him than she could have forbidden the sun to rise.

In a spiraling whirl, they clung together, temporarily losing themselves in each other as the sensual tension mounted. Case gripped her fiercely, crushing her breasts against the roughness of his chest, using his strength to set a pattern that lifted her higher and higher until she was begging him to terminate the enveloping desire threatening to consume her.

"Oh, please! *Please!*"

Her cry was both a command and a plea that seemed to arouse him even further. But still he held her to his rhythm, letting her twist and cling and arch beneath him but never letting her push him into the final frenzy.

"Tell me how much you want me," he ordered heavily, his tongue circling her ear and creating unbearable pleasure. "I can feel your need, but I want to hear you tell me about it!"

"I want you!" she moaned, her nails raking the length of his back in an agony of desire. "I want you so much!"

"Swear to me there won't be anyone else!" he went on inexorably, his voice raw.

"There is no one else! You know that, Case. You, of all people, know that!"

"As long as we're together I want exclusive rights. I couldn't stand it if I thought you would let another man have you like this!"

She didn't respond to that. She couldn't. She didn't even understand what he meant. How long did he mean to be her lover? Did he really think she could even contemplate this level of surrender with another man?

She gasped as he suddenly increased the pace, taking her with him on a headlong flight to the finish line, sweeping past it, with her in his arms, into a shivering culmination of their passion. For Kendra reality faded to an indistinguishable speck in the distance.

A long time later she became aware of a tender hand easing several curling tendrils of hair off her damp forehead. She stirred against the hard maleness and settled more deeply into the warmth.

"Oh, no, you don't." The words were an amused, indulgent chuckle above her head. "You're not going to go to sleep on me this time. I learned my lesson, young woman. This time we talk, first!"

Kendra yawned like a cat and ignored him until he shook her gently into sleepy-eyed alertness. "I mean it, honey," he said more seriously, as she would have nestled back against his chest. "There are things you and I have to discuss!"

"Like what?" she mumbled with a complete lack of interest, her fingers moving lazily along his chest.

"Stop that," he ordered with a muffled laugh. "You're tickling me."

"You probably deserve it." She shrugged, eyes closing again.

"Come on, I can see this is hopeless!"

"Where are we going?" she protested as he slid off the bed and reached down to pull her up beside him.

"We're going to take a shower and wake you up so that you're able to carry on a serious conversation!"

"I don't want to take a shower now," she explained carefully as he guided her toward the bathroom, which opened off her bedroom. She caught sight of the time as they passed a gold-and-glass-cased clock. "It's late!"

"It's not even midnight."

"I'm usually sound asleep by midnight!" she argued.

"Well, I'm not. It occurs to me that one of us is going to have to adjust to the other's schedule." He grinned good-naturedly as he switched on the light in the bathroom and glanced around. "Good Lord, even in here! You're as bad as I am when it comes to interior decorating! What's your private fantasy, honey? Going back a couple of hundred years to an age of ballrooms and royalty that probably never existed?"

"What's wrong with my bathroom?" she charged, coming awake at last to peer at the walls papered in a formal stripe in the traditional French Directoire colors of black and gold. A gold basin set in a marble counter and an elaborately carved gilt mirror added to the lush look.

"Nothing, as long as the plumbing isn't two hundred years old, also," he placated.

"I'll bet even the plumbing of two hundred years ago is better than what you're going to find on that South Seas island of yours when you eventually get there!"

"How did you know I was going?" he drawled, sweeping aside the gold shower curtain and thrusting her gently inside. "Here, put your hair under this cap or we'll be up all night drying it."

With a sigh, Kendra obeyed because it was easier that way. When the hot shower finally brought her awake she realized she wasn't the only one standing in it.

"Case," she asked abruptly, lifting her head finally and noting he had removed his velvet patch. "What happened to your eye?" At any other time she wouldn't have had the courage to ask such a personal question. But tonight it seemed all right for some reason.

"A knife fight in Singapore," he told her laconically and ignored her instinctive flinch, turning his face into the water with relish.

"What—what happened to the other guy?" she dared, her eyes flickering along his hard, tanned length.

"Don't ask," he advised, his lashes closed against the force of the water. "It was a long time ago."

"I thought you said you wanted us to talk," she muttered aggressively, as she realized she wasn't going to get an answer. Reality was coming back now, and she was beginning to assimilate the fact that she was standing in her shower with a man she would never have dreamed of associating with under normal circumstances.

"I do and we will," he confirmed, his mouth crooking slightly at the corner as he turned, soap in hand, and began to scrub her vigorously. "But we're going to talk about the present, not the past."

His soap-slickened hands moved over her intimately, sliding across her breasts and hips with the intimate, proprietary touch of a lover. Well, Kendra thought in confusion, that's what he is, isn't he? He'd made himself her lover. And what in hell was she going to do about it?

In spite of his obvious pleasure in bathing her, Case made no move to initiate another session in bed. Instead she was thoroughly rinsed and dried with one of her gold towels until her skin glowed.

When he finally released her, Kendra scurried out into the bedroom and found her quilted champagne-colored satin robe. She was safely wrapped in it, her hair brushed free down her back, when he emerged.

"You'd better go put on some coffee or something or we won't be getting much talking done after all," he told her meaningfully as he stood there surveying her.

His soft laugh followed her out of the room as she hurried away to follow his advice.

When he ambled into the country-style kitchen a few minutes later, he was wearing only the dark wool slacks. Barefoot, his black hair glistening, his naked chest still slightly damp in places, there was a fundamentally primitive look about him that made Kendra's mouth go dry.

"Cookies and milk?" He grinned skeptically as he spotted the small tray she had prepared.

"I keep them on hand for Jason," she told him loftily, carrying the tray past him into the formal dining room. In addition to the large table there was a smaller one by the bay window. She set her burden down on it and took one of the two graceful little chairs.

"Okay," he growled, taking the other seat and reaching for a chocolate-chip cookie, "who's Jason?"

She eyed him for a second. "He looks a bit like you," she finally announced. "Except his eyes are green. But he's got black hair, and he's—"

"I didn't ask for a description, I asked who he was," Case reminded her, his earlier humor fading.

"He's Donna's son. And he's five years old," she added for good measure, her eyes twinkling.

"Umph," he replied around a cookie. "So much for Jason. But talking about him does bring us to another issue. How involved are you with Donna and her problems?"

Kendra shrugged. "She looked me up when she decided to file for divorce. She wanted to stay out of Radburn's reach until everything was final. I've been keeping her location a secret."

"From Radburn?"

"And her mother."

"Her mother!"

"That's right. Her mother is quite upset that she's getting a divorce. She thinks the world of Austin Radburn. And Radburn, of course, encourages that attitude. He wants to hang on to Donna until she comes into her inheritance."

"I suppose Jason's presence complicates things. A man's got a right to his son. . . ."

"Jason's father is dead. He was killed shortly after Jason was born," Kendra said quietly.

"This is Donna's second marriage?"

"Yes."

"Poor kid. First a widow, and now she's going through a divorce," he murmured sympathetically.

Kendra said nothing. Men always felt protective toward Donna. It didn't particularly surprise her to find even a man as hard as Case feeling that way, too. She sipped her milk in silence.

"So Donna's afraid Austin will grab the kid and hold on to him until the money comes through?" Case went on after a moment, chewing another cookie reflectively.

"That's about it. Once she has the money she figures she'll be able to get out of his reach."

"Hmmm."

"I know," Kendra half-smiled at his tone. "I've had a few doubts about that myself. From what I know of Austin Radburn, he tends to be tenacious."

Case gave her a sidelong glance. "How much do you know of him?"

Kendra said coolly, "Not much, only that he owns a huge shipbuilding business in L.A.; that he virtually swept Donna off her feet when she came along. For a time he made her quite happy, I think. . . ."

"She didn't look too happy during the time when she was running up a tab at my place."

"No," Kendra agreed softly. "That was a very bad time for her. She almost"—she hesitated and then realized she shouldn't give away her cousin's secret—"she was very depressed. It was when she pulled herself out of it that she decided to get the divorce."

"What's worrying me," Case went on calmly, "is the sort of character Radburn sent to pump you for information. Why does he think you know where his wife is?"

"Donna and I were . . . very close before she married him," Kendra replied, her eyes on the cookie plate. "He knew that."

"Still, this is between him and his wife. I don't like the fact that you're involved," Case declared steadily.

"How could I say no when she asked me to help her?"

"I know, I know." He polished off the last of his milk. "I'll look into the matter in the morning."

"You'll what?" she snapped, startled. "Case, this doesn't concern you!"

"Don't say stupid things, honey, it doesn't fit your image." He smiled at her across the little table, a wicked, endearing smile that went very well with cookies and milk. "Just leave everything to me."

"Like hell!"

"A few minutes ago you were all soft and cuddly, and now you're turning feisty. Maybe I shouldn't have kept you up past your bedtime, after all," he chided lightly.

"Case, I mean it," she told him anxiously. "I don't want you getting involved in this!" Visions of him coolly ordering some underling like Wolf to "deal with Radburn" flashed into her mind. She still didn't know for certain what Wolf had done with Phelps! The casual implication of violence frightened her. Case Garrett frightened her.

"Let's find another subject," he suggested. "Shall I read you a bedtime story?"

"Case, please!"

"Don't look so scared, sweetheart. You've got nothing to worry about. I'll take care of it." He collected the glasses and the plate, stacked them on the tray, and stood up to carry them back to the kitchen.

Kendra stared after him, stricken. What had she unleashed by allowing him into her life? But how could she have kept him out of it? she asked herself helplessly.

As he disappeared confidently into the kitchen she leaped to her feet and followed, standing nervously in the doorway as he stacked the dishes in the dishwasher.

"Case, I want your word you won't do anything—anything—"

He looked up. "Anything what?" he prompted, and then his gaze slitted with understanding. "Anything . . . illegal? Is that what's worrying you?"

"Well, frankly, yes!"

"That's honest enough, I guess," he observed dryly, straightening. "I've scared you, haven't I?" He came forward before she could answer, pulling her into his arms and stroking his fingers through her hair. "Don't worry, honey," he whispered. "Please, don't worry."

"I am worried, Case," she mumbled into his bare shoulder. "You shouldn't have come here. You should never have come here!"

"Don't say that, Kendra. Not after what we just shared."

She stepped back, wrenching herself free from his hold. "That's still the only thing you can think about, isn't it? I must be out of my mind to be standing here trying to talk to you! Why don't you go back to your casino and your friends like Wolf Higgins! Please don't get me involved in your world. It scares me!"

His face hardened as he watched her anguished expression. "Can't you trust me, Kendra?"

"No," she said flatly, "I can't. I've got a long way to go in order to recover from what you did to me in Lake Tahoe. I don't want to let you do any more damage!"

"Kendra—"

"Will you please go, Case? You got what you came for!"

He took a step forward, and then stopped as she backed up immediately. There was pain in the look he gave her, but Kendra refused to let it sway her. She was already far too weak where this man was concerned. She thought he was going to say something else, but he clamped his teeth together almost audibly and walked around her, heading for the bedroom.

She waited tensely, not knowing what to expect. But he reappeared fully dressed and came toward her with a brisk, gliding stride.

"Good night, Kendra," he grated harshly, cupping the back of her neck and dropping a quick, hard kiss on her mouth. "I'll call you tomorrow."

"You don't know . . ." she began hopefully.

"Where you work?" he concluded violently. "Yes, I do. I know a great deal about you, and I'm learning more by the minute!"

"Case! Wait a minute! Where are you going? What are

you going to do?" she called after him as he headed for the door.

He paused, one hand on the knob, and told her tersely, "I'm going to a hotel, since I don't get the feeling I'm being welcomed here. As for what I'm going to do, I haven't decided yet. Wolf is taking care of things at the casino, so I've got a little time to figure out a course of action. Don't worry, you'll be the first to know when I make up my mind!"

A moment later he was gone, out into the cold, foggy night.

CHAPTER EIGHT

The phone rang at work the next day just after Kendra and Norris had seen the Richardson people happily out the door. Kendra had turned to her partner with a mutually congratulatory grin when Tina, the secretary, put the call through.

"Case!" Kendra exclaimed as Norris removed himself from her office with a speculative little lift of his eyebrows. She felt her heart pick up a beat as Case's deep, drawling voice greeted her.

"Good morning, honey. I'm calling for a couple of reasons—"

"If two of them are to apologize and reassure me that you'll stay out of my personal problems, I shall be delighted to take this call!"

There was a pause. "You sound a tad argumentative this morning. Annoyed with me for walking out last night?"

Kendra lifted her silently beseeching gaze toward the heavens and wondered why she was suddenly feeling very lighthearted. "What are the reasons for the call, Case?" she said with exaggerated patience. "And how did you find out where I work, anyhow?"

"I started with the guy you bought your return ticket from up in Lake Tahoe," he began helpfully.

"Those people aren't supposed to give out personal information!"

"I know."

There was a pregnant silence during which Kendra thought about such matters as bribery, intimidation, and people who could be bought. "Let's get back to the reasons for this call," she finally said politely.

"Right. The first is that I forgot to get Donna's phone number from you before I left last night."

"No kidding." Kendra decided she could be laconic, too.

"Come on, honey. Give. I told you I was going to look into her situation today." The dark voice was all soft cajolery.

"I'm not giving that number out to you, Austin Radburn, Gilbert Phelps, or anyone else who comes looking!"

"Kendra—"

"I'll call Donna," Kendra heard herself say placatingly. "If she wants to talk to you, I'll give her *your* number."

"No good. I think she'll be a little too shy to take the initiative," he told her with great certainty.

"Why? Oh, you mean because of the gambling debt?"

"Something like that," he agreed dryly. "Let me have the number, sweetheart, I don't want to waste time with an argument."

"No." She waited, chewing nervously on her lip, to see what he'd do next.

"Determined to be difficult, huh? Okay, if that's the way you want it. I'll get it myself," he told her cheerfully.

"How? It's unlisted."

"What do you want to bet it's neatly written down somewhere close to your phone at home?"

"I'll hide it as soon as I get home tonight!" she vowed.

"Too late. I'll be in and out long before that."

"What are you talking about?" Kendra frowned at the phone. "The door's locked, and Mrs. Colter doesn't have a key!" She added that last piece of news with a sense of triumph, pleased at having anticipated him.

126

"I don't need a key," he retorted calmly.

"Are you threatening to break into my flat?" she demanded, shocked in spite of what she already knew about this man.

"I won't break the door down, don't fret," he assured her sardonically.

"Case Garrett, if I get home tonight and find out you've illegally entered my flat, I'll—" Words failed her.

"Calm down, honey. If you're convinced I'm a member of the criminal element, at least give me credit for being good at my work. I promise it will be professionally done. There won't be a hint of evidence lying around for you to find. You'll never even know I've been there. *Wait a minute,*" he suddenly broke off to yell, sensing accurately that she was about to slam the receiver down in his ear. "There is a second reason for this call!"

"If it's anything like the first reason, I think I'll have you arrested on sight!"

"And you keep trying to tell me I broke your spirit that night in Lake Tahoe!" he muttered, sounding much aggrieved. "Where's all this fear of the male of the species you claim you rediscovered at my hands?"

Kendra held the phone away from her ear for an instant, realizing she was on the verge of laughter. What was happening to her? She was afraid of Case Garrett, wasn't she? She *ought* to be!

"You want me to be afraid of you?" she finally managed sweetly, still trying to sort through her own emotions.

"Well, maybe not fear," he conceded thoughtfully. "But a little healthy respect might be welcome! About my second reason. It has to do with dinner."

Kendra waited, knowing she should be jumping in, feet first, with a firm refusal yet unable to find the words.

"I'll pick you up around six-thirty," he concluded succinctly. "Have a good day, honey."

It was he who hung up the phone in her ear.

Kendra sat staring at the dead receiver, unwilling to admit aloud how intensely glad she was to find him still in pursuit. It was all wrong, naturally, but she couldn't shake off the sensation of excitement and laughter. She hadn't felt quite this way about a man in her entire life, let alone the past two years!

If only, she told herself sadly, circumstances were different. If only Case Garrett were a different man, say a proper San Francisco businessman or a lawyer. If only he hadn't shown her so graphically just how weak she still was. If only he weren't who he was . . .

For some reason, that made her think of his love of the South Seas. How had he come by it? Did he dream of returning some day? Perhaps he would retire there on the fortune he must be making at the casino. She understood about dreams. She understood about fantasy . . .

With a muttered imprecation Kendra dialed Donna's number. A realistic approach to life told her the odds were in favor of Case getting hold of her cousin's telephone number before the day was out.

"Case Garrett's trying to reach me? Oh, no! Kendra, don't let him! I couldn't bear to face him! I'm so ashamed!" Donna was wailing a moment later on the other end of the line.

"Ashamed? But, Donna," Kendra began, a little surprised at the reasoning behind the other woman's reaction. "There's no cause to be embarrassed. Lots of people run up gambling debts, and it's not as if you're not paying yours."

"You don't understand," Donna informed her heavily.

"So enlighten me!"

There was a long silence until finally Donna said quietly, "I offered to pay my debts shortly after I lost all that money."

"How?" Kendra was suddenly experiencing a deep

128

sense of foreboding. She began to rapidly put two and two together, and she didn't like the sum.

"How do you think?" Donna groaned. "I offered to go to bed with him in exchange for the IOUs. He refused. I feel so humiliated that I made the offer!"

"I see." Kendra couldn't think of anything to say. Eventually she realized she should offer some comfort. "It's all right, though, Donna. He seems to understand that you might be embarrassed about facing him. He says he wants to help. The real problem is that his kind of help could cause a much more serious situation than you've already got."

"Why?" Donna sounded genuinely curious.

"Donna! What do we know of him? The man runs a gambling casino, for God's sake! He's got a rather mysterious past, to say the least, and you ought to meet some of his employees! One of them is named Wolf, which ought to tell you something, and he took care of that poor Gilbert Phelps, and I still don't know what happened to the man!"

"I wish Austin could be made to fade from the scene that conveniently," Donna noted practically.

"Oh, my God, Donna. You don't know what you're saying!"

"Relax, cousin," the younger woman soothed. "You sound like you're really down on Garrett. Not turning into a snob by any chance, are you?"

"Listen to me, Donna," Kendra began seethingly, "I'm going to wash my hands of this whole mess if you don't behave sensibly!"

"Jason! Cut that out," Donna yelled at that moment. Then she spoke quickly, apologetically into the phone. "I've got to run, Kendra. Let's just see what happens with Case. Maybe it wouldn't be such a bad idea to talk to him. There might be possibilities in the situation now that I think about it."

For the second time that morning Kendra hung up the phone with mixed emotions. Among them was a growing feeling of being trapped in a situation rapidly escalating out of her control. Perhaps it was *she* who ought to fade from the scene.

When Case arrived at the front door of the flat that evening, Kendra met him with fiercely accusing eyes.

"Well?"

"Well, what?" he countered pleasantly, sweeping with his eyes her slender figure sheathed in an elegantly simple gown of deep, vibrant burgundy. A flounce of pleats at the knee lent a note of charm to the otherwise austere cut. Her hair was in a sophisticated chignon, and the small diamonds in her ears glittered.

Case's gaze reflected undisguised male approval. Dressed in his usual dark colors accented with the crisp whiteness of a handmade shirt, he appeared dangerously attractive to Kendra as he stood politely at her door. She had an almost overpowering urge to run her fingertips through the hint of silver moonlight that rippled in his hair.

"Did you break in here today?" she challenged aggressively.

"Does anything look disturbed? Is there any evidence of someone having gained forcible entry?"

"You did, didn't you? Did you call Donna?"

"We'll talk about that later," he consoled lightly, helping her into the white mink. He ran a hand through the soft fur as he settled it on her shoulders, and his next words came in an entirely different tone.

"I've got to ask you something, honey. And it's probably going to make you mad as hell. Humor me, please."

"What's the question?" she asked suspiciously.

"If you haven't had a serious relationship with anyone else for the past two years, who's paying for all this?" His gesture indicated everything from the diamonds in her ears to the sumptuous furnishings, and his expression was too·intense to shrug off.

"I am," she stated proudly, truthfully. "Every cent is from the agency. And you're right. I'm furious!"

"I had to be sure. . . ." His slightly roughened palms cupped her face, and she saw the flood of satisfied relief in his dark gaze as he bent to kiss her with unleashed passion that instantly drained her anger. Before she could recover her voice he took her hand and led her toward the door.

"I will say one thing about San Franciscans," Case said, grinning, half an hour later as they were seated in the posh, dimly lit bar of the waterfront restaurant. "They know how to dress well and eat well!"

"We have our priorities," Kendra murmured demurely as she turned to gaze out at the night-darkened sweep of San Francisco Bay. There was an unconscious satisfaction in her response that served to broaden Case's smile.

She turned her head and encountered his warm look. "You seem to know some of our best places, though," she admitted, referring to the expensive restaurant, replete with old-style West Coast opulence.

"I cheated," he confessed with a wry grin. "I know the owner."

"Ah." She sipped her glass of wine and favored him with a calculating smile.

"Don't say it," he begged dryly.

"Would I be so gauche as to question your association with the owner of this place? I'm sure it's an entirely *professional* relationship. Which brings us to the business of how you obtained Donna's phone number," she concluded smoothly.

"Could we," he asked very steadily, "talk about something else this evening?"

"Such as?"

"Such as us?" His next words came with an appallingly

stark clarity. "I want you, Kendra Loring. I wanted you the moment I saw you. And I don't mean for a few nights or an occasional fling here in San Francisco. I want you to come live with me."

The wine in Kendra's glass sloshed perilously close to the rim as she tried desperately to recover her fragmented poise. She could only stare speechlessly at him, unable to fully grasp the implication of what he was saying but knowing her whole life was threatening to come undone.

Case's mouth quirked whimsically, and he touched his fingers to the fine fabric of her burgundy dress. "You have everything, haven't you? A beautiful home, designer clothes, good jewelry, an excellent career. And I would like very much to take you away from all that."

"Take me where, Case? To a casino?" she managed faintly, still trying to work out a response. She felt literally staggered.

"No, to an island. An island in the South Seas."

"Your fantasy island?" she breathed.

"I'm buying a hotel there, Kendra. There's no casino attached. It's a small place, but very, very beautiful. The whole island is something out of a dream: Palm trees, sparkling water, endless beaches, friendly people, and enough wealthy tourists to make the hotel a paying proposition. Will you come and share it with me, Kendra?"

"Case, I—I don't know what to say. I'm stunned. I had no idea—" She broke off, awash in confusion. Her common sense said everything should be simple. The obvious answer was an unqualified no. But she'd never been asked to share a dream before. And she would never have imagined that a man like this would ask her to do so. Her dreams and goals had always been private.

He leaned forward, his hand covering one of hers. "Relax, honey." He shook his head. "I seem to say that to you a lot, don't I? But it's still good advice. Relax and stop trying to find a polite way to say no. I wouldn't accept it, anyway. We'll come back to the subject another time. I just wanted you to know where we're heading."

She fought for a semblance of cool control, seizing at the suggestion of a change of subject. She needed time to recover!

"If you've been wanting to run an island hotel, how did you wind up with a Nevada casino?"

"I sort of inherited it a few years ago," he explained, lifting one shoulder dismissively.

"A—a relative left it to you?"

"No, a friend. Someone for whom I worked and for whom I once did a favor."

"It must have been some favor!"

"I saved his life a long time ago. He took a liking to me; gave me a job. I think he began to think of me as the son he'd never had. And I know he definitely became something like a father to me. My parents died when I was very young. He was quite a man. I'll tell you about him someday."

"But not tonight?" she guessed perceptively.

"No, not tonight. He would have liked you, though. He liked people who have courage." Case smiled again with a strange, reminiscent look.

"Do you think I have courage?" she asked neutrally.

"By the truckload. I know I put a dent in your self-confidence the other night, but you'll get over that. It didn't affect your courage one bit. I know that much about you," he went on slowly. "I also know you've surrounded yourself with your own particular brand of fantasy. Where did you acquire a taste for eighteenth-century drawing-room furniture? How does that fit with training yourself in an exotic form of self-defense? And where did you learn that trick of pulling yourself in on yourself the way you did that night in Tahoe when you thought I was going to hurt you? You scared the hell out of me," he admitted. "I could feel you slipping away. . . ." His face hardened in recollection.

Kendra watched him for a moment, knowing she wanted to talk to him and at the same time telling herself she shouldn't give in to the temptation. But she couldn't resist.

"I've been on my own a long time," she began distantly. "My parents died in a car accident when I was in high school. I went to live with Donna's folks until I left for college, but although Donna and I grew close, I always felt like a guest in her parents' house. Somewhere along the line it struck me that I had only myself to depend on in life. Ultimately that's all any of us has, I suppose. Whatever I wanted I was going to have to create for myself."

Case nodded and she knew he understood.

"It seemed to me that there was no reason not to fill my life with whatever satisfied me. I discovered a love of coming back from work to a home that took me into another era. I liked the feeling of wearing good clothes. I liked having control over my work environment."

"So you simply went out and made what you wanted out of life." Case eyed her admiringly. "Don't you realize what sort of courage that takes? You're amazing!"

Kendra blinked, a little surprised. She'd never considered it amazing.

"What happened two years ago didn't break you," Case went on coolly. "You realized that one of the things you wanted from life was being able to live it without fear, so you went out and learned how not to be a victim."

"Some people would say I lost something important in the process . . ."

"You mean the ability to enjoy a normal, loving relationship? No, you didn't lose it. You simply put it under wraps for a while, waiting, I like to think, for the right man to come along and unwrap it again."

Kendra told herself she would have given a great deal

to wipe that look of smug male satisfaction off his smiling face, but she didn't quite know how.

"We belong together, Kendra Loring. We understand each other on a very fundamental level. We have a lot in common, even if it isn't obvious on the surface. We have basic views of life that are almost identical. It's what you make of it. We've come a long way on our own. Together we could do anything we wanted."

Kendra could find nothing to say to that. Unwillingly she remembered that flash of recognition she had experienced the first time she had seen him. Was that what it had been? A sense of finding a kindred spirit? No, that was too fantastic to credit. . . .

He danced with her after dinner, holding her close in an embrace that was simultaneously sensual and tender but which conveyed utterly his deep desire for her. She let herself be melded to the hard strength in him and wondered irrationally how a man like this could have such an instinctive knowledge of passion and gentleness when he took a woman in his arms.

Later he walked her through the bustle that was Fisherman's Wharf at night, people watching with her and seeming to enjoy the chaotic array of curio shops, hot-dog stands, restaurants of every description, and endless piles of crabs waiting for the cooking pot.

"It reminds me of a cleaned-up version of some of the places I used to know in the Far East," he told her at one point, chuckling. "Much safer, though."

She felt a pang as his words reminded her of the knife fight in Singapore, when he'd lost his left eye. She shivered.

When he drove her back to the flat in his black-and-silver Porsche, Kendra prepared herself to bid him a polite but firm good night. She needed time to think; time to sort through all the emotions he had drawn from her this evening.

But as if he knew exactly what she was thinking, Case denied her the time. When she turned on her doorstep it was too late. He crowded her gently into the room, shutting the door behind him and reaching for her before she could find the words to stop him.

"I know, I know," he consoled wryly as he unbelted the coat and slipped it off her shoulders. "If I were a gentleman, I would wait for an invitation. But I don't feel like arguing tonight, sweetheart. I want you too badly."

"Case, I need time to think . . ." she began urgently, appealingly, but she knew it was hopeless. Already she could feel his spell extending outward, binding her to him. It was getting easier for him, she reflected, her mind whirling as he dragged her against him and buried his hands in her hair, pulling it loose.

He didn't answer, swinging her high into his arms as her hair cascaded down. She met the lambent fire of his gaze and was unable to prevent the rising tide of her own response. It had been ebbing and flowing all evening, and now it was reaching its peak.

Her senses swam in a dazzling haze as he undressed her with long, sensual movements, and she found herself returning the beginning of the loveplay. She felt his fingers tremble with the force of his desire as he cupped her breast, and it made her moan thickly in response as she sank against his bare chest.

"You're going to have to come live with me on my island, Kendra," he growled, settling her onto the fur and lowering his weight beside her. "I can't do without you now!"

"Oh, Case . . ."

He sealed her mouth with a kiss that grew steadily more demanding, more enticing, more beguiling, as she responded. After a moment Kendra put all thoughts of the future out of her head once more and gave herself up to the need in both of them.

He made love to her as if he were unwrapping treasure, kissing her from her ankles to her ears, burying his face in the softness of her hair. Her body began to burn as he touched her everywhere until she could bear it no longer, but she knew she must give him the same pleasure in return.

He looked at her with such flaming need and longing when she levered herself up beside him and began exploring his body with her lips that Kendra could have wept. Nothing mattered here in the darkness but satisfying his desire.

She scorched kisses down his throat, her fingers threading through the hair of his chest. And then her tongue was tasting the skin of his stomach and thighs. The masculine roughness of him excited her, and he groaned deeply in his chest as she dampened him with her mouth.

Kendra felt his hands in her long hair, tugging her gently up the length of his body until she lay stretched out on top of him.

"Make love to me," he ordered huskily as he pulled her to him. "Put out this fire you've started. . . ."

She came to him, her softness flowing over him in a wave. His elemental pleasure in her was intoxicating to Kendra, and she wondered how she could be so certain making love would never be like this with any other man. Alone here with him on the soft fur it was easy to believe her imagination when it told her this man was the missing factor in her life.

He held her fiercely as the tide of their lovemaking reached its zenith, and she heard his half-stifled cry of satisfaction just as she herself was shaken by the small convulsion. They clung together, drifting in a world that held only themselves.

It was later, much later, just before she fell asleep in his arms, that Kendra felt Case stir vaguely and yawn.

"I almost forgot to tell you," he mumbled, folding her

closer. "We're meeting Donna and her son for dinner tomorrow night down in Chinatown. I think I've got things worked out."

"You did get her number and call her today, didn't you?" Kendra whispered.

"Yes."

She said nothing as he went to sleep beside her. But she thought about her cousin and how men always wanted to protect her. She lay awake quite a while thinking about it.

That memory was still in Kendra's mind the next evening as Case escorted her through the crowds on Grant Avenue. On every side shops featuring exotic wares from fine lacquered Oriental furniture to fantastic dragon kites drew tourists and locals like a magnet. The lantern street-lights, Oriental architectural trim on the buildings, and bustling shops and restaurants constituted the public face of a Chinese community numbering over thirty-six thousand people within its confines. Kendra knew only too well that much of the wealth generated from the tourist trade never managed to trickle down to the bulk of the district's population.

But Chinatown was still Chinatown, a gaudy, exciting, glittering slice of another world. And the food could border on the fabulous.

"I told Donna to take a cab to this address. She and Jason should be here by now," Case remarked, guiding Kendra up a flight of stairs to a poorly marked restaurant on the second floor of a building.

"Case, I wish you would tell me exactly what you're planning," Kendra told him for the hundredth time that day. She was a bundle of nerves this evening, she realized. She knew he was taking over, and she didn't know how to stop him.

"I will. Over dinner. Ah-hah! That must be Jason."

Kendra looked up to find a smiling, relaxed-looking

138

Donna waiting in the small restaurant lobby, Jason bouncing impatiently by her side. The little boy stopped bouncing to stare in open-mouthed fascination at Case's black velvet patch. Case gave him a slow, buccaneerish grin, and Jason became an instant admirer. Kendra had a fleeting thought that with his black hair, the little boy could have passed for Case's own son.

Jason leaped to his feet and rushed forward to stand gazing up at his new hero. His mother smiled ruefully as her son asked with great interest, "Are you the one who's going to take Mom and me to Lake Tahoe?"

Kendra turned stunned eyes on her cousin as Case dropped to his haunches and ruffled the little boy's hair.

"Would you like that?" he said to the child.

Jason's vigorous glee was answer enough. "Can I play in the snow? I've never seen snow!"

"I don't see why not."

"What's going on?" Kendra said evenly, glancing from Case to Donna in chilled anxiety.

"Let's go and eat," Case told her, straightening. "We'll explain it all to you over dinner. I'm starved." He gave her a level look that warned very plainly against making a scene.

Half an hour later Donna looked up from her plate of beef in black bean sauce and smiled at her cousin. "So you see, Kendra, this plan of Case's should solve everything nicely. It will get Jason and me out of your hair, and it should cool Austin's enthusiasm to come looking for us once he knows we've got—friends." The last word came out a little lamely, and Donna's eyes flew briefly to Case's wry gaze.

"You mean protection." Kendra used her chopsticks very deftly on her cod in ginger sauce. She avoided looking at either of the other two. "You're going to call Austin when you arrive and let him know you're still going through with the divorce and that you're no longer vulnerable, is that it?" she summarized.

"That's it," Case agreed meaningfully, munching his stir-fried rice noodles. "Any objections?" he added challengingly.

Kendra sighed and shook her head. "It's Donna's decision," she stated quietly.

"Once he knows where I am he won't send people like Phelps after you," Donna pointed out enthusiastically, and then she suddenly sobered abruptly as Kendra continued to focus on her food. "Or—or were you secretly hoping he would come looking in person, Kendra?"

Kendra glanced up sharply, pinning her anxious-looking cousin with a cold hazel glare. "No."

The tension around the table seemed to erupt in full force, stilling everyone's movements, even Jason's. The little boy looked uncomprehendingly at his elders, and then went very quietly back to his noodles.

"I'm sorry, Kendra," Donna whispered apologetically. "I didn't mean that—"

"What's this all about?" Case interrupted in a deadly tone that neither woman could ignore.

"I don't wish to discuss it," Kendra tried grimly, knowing it was hopeless.

Case turned a cold, pointed glance on Donna, who wilted immediately.

"Before Kendra introduced me to Austin the two of them were seeing a—great deal of each other," she explained carefully. "He came to San Francisco often."

"Donna, please . . . !"

But under Case's forceful prompting, Donna kept talking, the apology in her voice quite clear. "Austin took one look at me and swept me off my feet. At the time I felt guilty for taking him away from Kendra. But I was in love, or so I thought. Later I realized he'd only married me for the inheritance. He needs the money to shore up

140

a flagging business, you see. I've told Kendra she should be grateful she didn't marry him, but sometimes—"

"Enough! We'll talk about it later," Case gritted.

Kendra shivered at the unleashed savagery in his voice. She had an almost overwhelming urge to explain everything, but there was no way. Not then.

It was Jason who pulled the three stricken adults back to the present. He licked his fingers and reached for a fortune cookie.

"Kendra's been teaching me tricks," he announced to Case. "Do you know any tricks?"

Case looked at Kendra, and she could feel the waves of his jealousy lapping dangerously at her body. "What kind of tricks?"

"Tricks for bashing people," Jason explained cheerfully. "Like on TV." He turned to Kendra. "Will you teach me another one tonight when we go home?"

Kendra looked steadily at the dark, threatening man across the table.

"Why don't you ask Case to teach you some of his tricks," she said very deliberately to the boy. "He knows more than I do."

Jason's opinion of Case obviously ascended another couple of notches as his green eyes sparkled. "Do you? More tricks than Kendra, even?"

Case drew in his breath, wrenching his gaze away from Kendra's taut features and turning back to the child. "I know some different ones," he said slowly. "And I've had a little more experience."

"Will you show me?" Jason appealed, eyes wide and excited.

Case appeared to come to some inner conclusion before he said coolly, "I'll show you each one tonight after dinner."

"Yippee!"

"What's the matter, Kendra?" Case chided over the

sound of Jason's delighted response, "aren't you excited, too?"

"You forget," she reminded him with acid sweetness. "You've already shown me some of your tricks."

"I'll teach you the counter move to the one I showed you last time," he told her quietly.

And he did, but not until he'd taught Jason a surprisingly effective little karate kick that thoroughly enchanted the boy. He ran around his mother's apartment kicking everything in sight and concluding with a daring attack on Case's shin that landed with unexpected impact. Case had been involved in a serious discussion of plans for the drive to Lake Tahoe at the time.

In spite of her uneasy mood Kendra couldn't help but giggle as the little boy landed his blow with an audible thud. He accompanied it with a very proper shout. Case's muffled oath turned Kendra's giggle into outright laughter.

"I can see it's time for lesson number two," Case told a mischievous-eyed Jason.

"What's that?" the boy asked eagerly.

"That's the one where you learn not to use your new-found skill in a foolhardy fashion. Try that kick again."

Jason ran forward with delight, lashing out with the well-aimed heel of his foot, and promptly found himself dangling upside down as Case held him by one ankle and finished the discussion with Donna.

Kendra's lesson came after a near-silent drive back to her flat. Her nerves were keyed to a feverish pitch by the time Case took the key and inserted it in the door of her flat. She wondered how to tell him about Austin, and in the next breath reminded herself she didn't owe this man any explanations. But she waited for him to demand them, knowing it was going to be almost impossible to refuse.

It wasn't Austin he brought up first, however, as he

142

closed the door behind him. Case helped her off with her coat and then spun her around to face him.

"About your lesson . . ." he began quietly.

"I'm—I'm not really in the mood," Kendra tried hesitantly, not knowing what to expect from him while he was in the grip of jealousy.

"Pay attention," he ordered briefly. A moment later she was flat on her back, pinned beneath him just as she had been that night in Lake Tahoe.

"Case, please, don't . . . !" The fear surged through her. Was this the way he was going to take out his anger over her relationship with Austin?

He ignored her plea and started giving terse, blunt instructions. Almost at once the fear receded. He wasn't going to hurt her. Kendra began to listen as he grimly and concisely taught her what she needed to know to dislodge him.

When the lesson was over he rolled to one side and lay looking up at the ceiling.

"Do you love him?"

"No," she said quietly, lying beside him on the Oriental rug. It was the truth, and perhaps it showed in her voice, because she felt rather than heard the long sigh of relief he gave.

"God, if you only knew what I went through this evening after Donna mentioned him, wondering if you were only helping her in order to have another chance with Radburn." He groaned, turning to pull her into his arms. "I have to have you, Kendra. I couldn't let you go to another man. Not now."

His mouth came down passionately on hers, and Kendra was saved from blurting out the clamoring truth that was suddenly assailing her from all sides.

She was in love with this man.

CHAPTER NINE

The following morning Kendra delayed her departure for the office in order to see the small Lake Tahoe–bound party on its way. She stood on the sidewalk in front of her flat and watched Jason jumping around inside Case's Porsche beside Donna.

His mother was trying unsuccessfully to calm him. Case was inside Kendra's apartment, collecting his shaving gear and his clothes, and that small action had not gone unnoticed by Donna.

"Kendra," she began, giving up on Jason for the moment, "I hadn't realized you and Case—" She looked up through the open window, her lovely eyes wide and questioning.

Kendra gave her a wry glance. "Don't ask for an explanation. I haven't got one. At least not one that makes any sense. I never intended—"

"I'm delighted!" Donna interrupted, grinning warmly. "Good lord, cousin! It's been nearly two years since you last showed any interest at all in a man! I'm just a little startled to know you've succumbed so quickly and so completely. Especially to a man you were going out of your way to warn me about because of his, er, questionable background!"

"A warning that you've paid no attention to." Kendra sighed, wondering again at the wisdom of what Donna was doing. Kendra had no doubt her cousin would get the

145

protection she wanted up in Lake Tahoe, but there was such a thing as overkill. She bit her lip. Under the circumstances that didn't seem like an especially good word to use.

"I trust Case. I'll admit I was a little nervous yesterday when he called, but after we talked for a few minutes I realized he only wanted to help. I didn't understand quite *why* he should want to go out of his way for someone who owes him as much money as I do, but when I saw him with you last night it all became very clear! He certainly can turn on the charm when he wants to, can't he?" Donna concluded admiringly.

"I've been on my guard since I first walked into his casino," Kendra confessed. "I never intended to even like him, let alone be charmed by him! Now look at me!"

"Still worried about becoming a *gangster's woman?*" Donna teased mercilessly, laughing up at her.

"Donna! Don't say things like that!"

"I'm only kidding."

"Are you? Personally there are moments when I'm terrified!" Which wasn't precisely true, Kendra had to admit privately. But when she got to thinking too deeply about Case's career, she did get nervous.

"Why? Afraid he'll beat you if you step out of line?" Donna grinned.

Kendra dismissed that joking question with an impatient wave of her hand. "No, it's not that. But, Donna, what do I know about him?"

"What do you need to know? I knew a great deal about Austin Radburn. Mom was thrilled when I announced my marriage to him, because the Radburn name is old and respected. She still refuses to believe he was only marrying me for the inheritance, and she won't listen when I try to tell her how he treated Jason and me. She says I'm being selfish and irrational. You'd have to have lived with the man to know just how insidiously cruel he could be. But

I can't say I didn't know a lot about him when I married him! I knew what clubs he belonged to, knew the history of his family, knew the people he associated with, knew about his shipbuilding business—Oh, I knew everything that counted. And look what good it did me!" Donna's mouth twisted with remembered bitterness.

"It's over now, Donna. Don't think about it. You're doing the right thing, taking hold of your own life!"

"Not any too soon, either." Donna groaned, glancing at Jason, who was playing with the steering wheel. "And I owe it all to this little guy. I was on a real downhill slide for a while there, Kendra. When I woke up in the hospital the morning after I took those sleeping pills, Jason was the first thing I thought of. I finally understood that I couldn't destroy myself and leave him alone. He needed me. And the first thing I had to do was get both of us out of the reach of Austin Radburn. I did you a favor by distracting him from you, Kendra. Please believe me!"

Kendra thought about that. Would she have ever married Austin if things had progressed differently?

"All set?"

Case's crisp words cut through Kendra's thoughts, and she stepped back from the Porsche as he walked toward her. His black hair was damp from the shower, his velvet patch back in place. He was dressed in slacks and a long-sleeved yellow shirt, open at the throat. He looked very good to her in the watery sunlight of a young San Francisco morning.

"Jason can't wait to get started." Kendra smiled as Case's long, gliding stride brought him to a point directly in front of her.

"Jason can wait long enough for me to say good-bye, can't you, Jason?" Case tossed the shaving kit in through the window, and the little boy yelled happily, grabbing for it. Donna turned to keep the razor out of Jason's questing fingers, and Case turned to catch Kendra's shoulders tightly in his hands.

He pulled her gently out of immediate earshot of the occupants of the Porsche and stood for a moment gazing down intently into her strained features. Kendra tried to summon a casual smile. What would he have said if she'd lost her head completely last night and confessed her love for him?

No, as strangely ambivalent as she felt about his going, it was for the best. She needed time, Kendra told herself, even as she searched his taut expression. Time to assess the situation and the risks she was on the verge of taking. She had to decide what she really wanted out of life. Because once she had made up her mind, she would be committed. What was worrying her was the awful premonition that the commitment had already been made.

"I'll be back in a couple of days," Case drawled softly. She felt his fingers gripping her with barely concealed urgency, and there was an equally urgent longing in his dark eye. "When I get Donna and Jason settled I'll return and we can make our plans."

"What's the hurry, Case?" she asked pleadingly, sensing that the time she wanted was going to be wrenched out of her hands.

"I can't wait very long for you, sweetheart," he told her deeply.

She flushed. "I hadn't noticed you doing much waiting," she had to say pointedly.

A wry humor played about the edges of his mouth, and one black brow lifted sardonically. "Knowing I can make you want me in bed isn't quite enough, honey. I need a sense of security; a little reassurance. I'm looking for a *commitment*, Kendra Loring. One hundred percent; total. And what's more, I think you know it. That's why you've got that slightly panicked look in your eyes this morning, isn't it?"

"If I do, you ought to feel guilty for having caused it!" she retorted spiritedly.

His thumbs worked lazy circles on her shoulders, moving across her white cashmere pullover in a way that made her tingle.

"I refuse to feel guilty if the end result is to stampede you into coming away with me." He chuckled wickedly, leaning down to fasten his mouth on hers in a fierce, swift kiss that perfectly conveyed the impression of a man who was regretting having to leave his woman behind even for a couple of days.

Kendra felt quite breathless when he let her go to stride around the front of the Porsche.

"Move over, Jason," Case ordered easily. "We've got a long drive ahead of us, and there are one or two things we should get clear before we depart."

"Good-bye, Kendra." Donna leaned out to smile once more as Jason was settled down. "Take care, and I'll phone Austin as soon as I arrive to make sure he keeps his private detectives away from you!"

"Thanks. I—I hope this is what you want, Donna. . . ."

"Oh, I feel much more comfortable having a man take charge," Donna said airily with obvious honesty. Kendra knew her cousin spoke the truth. Donna was always happier knowing she could trust herself to the care of a man. Kendra had always had to take care of herself. She would never be the dependent, clinging kind, and she knew it.

Kendra caught Case's glance as he turned the key in the ignition.

"Good-bye," she whispered.

"I'll be back," he told her a little roughly, as if he were holding back a more emotional statement.

She watched them drive off into early-morning traffic, and with a pang realized how much like a family they all looked. Donna was happier than she had appeared in a long time. Her cousin felt safe again. And Jason couldn't have been more delighted with life. He didn't remember his father, and Austin had certainly never been more than a large, intimidating figure in his young life. Case Garrett was a whole new breed of adult male, and Jason liked him.

Grimly Kendra forced herself away from such thoughts. She had to make some decisions. Unless, of course, the decision was taken out of her hands during the long drive to Lake Tahoe when Case would have nothing to do but talk to a lovely, appealingly helpless Donna. Unhappily Kendra remembered what had happened the last time she had introduced her cousin to a man. . . .

That morning, she threw herself into her work, dictating a pile of letters that were to keep Tina busy all day. When Norris silently invited a comment or two on the man who had been waiting for her in Mrs. Colter's flat, she ignored him. He took the hint, knowing Kendra fairly well after so many years of partnership.

By midafternoon she was exhausted, and the thought of having to go out again that evening was disheartening. But business was business. She drank another cup of tea and wondered if Donna and Jason had arrived yet in Tahoe. Where would they stay? In the fantasy room over the casino?

The phone was ringing much later that evening when she let herself into the flat. As she picked it up she had the feeling it had been ringing for a long time. And she knew who it was before he spoke.

"It's nearly eleven," Case observed coolly. "Where have you been?"

"Out," she managed to retort flippantly, thinking of the long day he had just spent with Donna. There was an uncomfortable silence, and to her disgust she heard herself adding dryly, "With Norris and some clients. Business, I'm afraid."

"Is he there?" Case demanded softly.

"Who? Norris? No, it was my turn to take him home this evening. We split the chore of driving on these occasions," she told him calmly. "How was the trip?"

He hesitated, and she could sense him trying to make up his mind about whether or not to push the subject of her business dates with Norris. If she was so foolish as to go away with him, Kendra told herself, she would have to be prepared for a very possessive lover. Instinct told her Case Garrett would take all or nothing.

"The trip was fine," he finally said, opting, apparently, not to berate her long distance. She wondered wryly at his restraint. "Jason's finally gone to bed. Wolf had a job keeping him out of the casino this evening!"

Kendra thought about the homey little scene and sighed. "Was he thrilled with the snow?"

"He was; Wolf wasn't."

"Wolf?"

"Jason had him hitched to a sled within an hour of our arrival!"

"That figures. How did Wolf take it?"

"Surprisingly well. He's the one who got Jason into bed a few minutes ago. His mother couldn't do a thing with him, he was so wound up. Tomorrow I'm moving them into a nearby apartment. Wolf's going to keep an eye on them."

"Oh. Did—did Donna call Radburn?"

"First thing," Case assured her promptly. "She told him where she was, who he would have to see to get to her, and that she fully intended to go through with the divorce. He knows she's not vulnerable any longer. I think he'll have the sense to give it up."

"And if he doesn't?" Kendra asked evenly.

She could almost see him shrug on the other end. "If he shows up, he'll be dealt with. If he's got the sense to leave Donna alone, he can go his own way. It doesn't make much difference to me. I just wanted him to realize there's no point in asking you questions through guys like Phelps."

Kendra remained silent.

"Kendra?"

"Hmmm?"

"Have you thought about us?"

"Yes," she admitted. "But don't ask for a decision over the phone, Case. I need time. You must know you're turning my world upside down by asking me to go away with you."

"I know," he murmured. "But that's what you did to me when you walked into my casino that night. Are you still angry at me for what I did to you? Is that why you won't give me an answer?"

"What would you do if I said yes?" she drawled, inspired by a sudden spark of mischief. "Get down on your hands and knees and beg me to forgive you?"

"Well, that's one option, I suppose," he conceded with a considering air. She knew he'd picked up on her sudden burst of recklessness.

"You've got another?" she invited.

"Yes, but it's for emergency use only," he told her deliberately.

"And highly illegal, I'll bet!"

"As hell. But don't worry about me. You know I don't leave evidence behind."

"How *did* you get into my flat yesterday to get Donna's number?"

"Sorry, I don't divulge professional secrets." He chuckled laconically.

"You gave me that lesson in self-defense last night," she reminded him.

"I must have gone nuts. I'll be in a bind if you decide to use it on me, won't I?"

"Are you going to tell me you taught me something

against which you don't have a defense?" she scoffed dryly.

"You'll never know unless you decide to use it, will you?" he noted cheerfully.

"Case," she said suddenly, intently, "this is crazy. You know that, don't you? People just don't leave everything behind and go off to live on an island!"

"Most people don't," he agreed. "Probably because they haven't got the courage to do it. I'll see you in a couple of days, honey. Good night, and don't open the door to any strangers."

"Good night, Case." Kendra replaced the receiver with a tremulous little sigh. The lovely room seemed much cooler without the sound of his voice.

As she slowly, methodically undressed for bed she wondered why she couldn't summon up the fierce resentment she ought to feel toward him. He *had* destroyed something important to her that night in Tahoe when he'd shown her how vulnerable she still was.

But she was beginning to think that it wasn't the fact that he'd countered her attack that had bothered her. The churning resentment that had burned in her mind during the flight home had been because he'd shown her the depths of a new and previously unsuspected vulnerability. Once one recovered from the dent in the ego, one could accept the rational fact that there were more dangerous people in the world. What had been far more unnerving was the discovery that one could find oneself so deeply attracted to a man who lived by a fundamentally different code.

And, Kendra decided as she lay staring at the darkened ceiling, she mustn't kid herself. Case had come to his present success via a much different route than she had taken. She didn't want to think of him as a man who lived by his own law. She was terrified of all that that implied. What would become of her if she gave herself to such a

153

man? She shuddered at Donna's teasing words: *A gangster's woman.*

No, she told herself wildly, flinging around to pound her pillow. He wasn't! He couldn't be! Or at least he must be reformed by now. After all, he did run a legal business. . . .

She gritted her teeth and tried not to think about it. Like an ostrich, she wanted to hide from the possibility of what Case might be or what he might once have been.

It was a long time before she fell asleep.

She was no nearer a decent rationalization the next morning when she returned to the office. For the sake of her co-workers she forced herself to bury her conflicting moods, which would have wrecked havoc in the small office. It took an amazing amount of will to perform the feat, but she congratulated herself at having been successful as she finished signing the last of the letters she'd dictated to Tina.

Norris wandered in around four o'clock from an appointment with a client.

"Think I'll take off early today," he announced. "I'm feeling lousy."

"Coming down with something?" Kendra asked sympathetically, lifting her gaze from a new stack of résumés that had arrived in the mail.

"Maybe," he admitted. He did look a little dragged out, she thought. "I'll go home and pop a few aspirin and get some rest. That should knock it out of my system, with any luck. Everything okay here? I think we're on top of most of it, don't you?"

"Yes," she agreed, glancing at the folders on her desk. "I'll finish going through these and get them ready for Tina to catalog and file. I think the Richardson people will be pleased at the selection we've got for them."

"Good. I'll see you in the morning. Hopefully!"

She watched her partner leave, and then turned back to

the résumés. An hour later Tina stuck her head around the door to say good-bye.

"I'll get busy doing the workups on those tomorrow morning. Mind if I leave early on Friday?"

Kendra smiled. "Got plans for the weekend?"

"Skiing up at Tahoe," Tina told her happily.

Kendra's smile faded. "That sounds like fun. Sure, you can leave early tomorrow." Was the whole world revolving around Tahoe these days?

"Great. Thanks, Kendra. See you in the morning."

Kendra sighed to herself as the office fell silent. It was time she got ready to leave. With her thoughts running back and forth between work and Case Garrett, it was a cinch she wasn't going to accomplish anything particularly useful by staying late.

She was stacking folders and making some effort to leave a neat work space when the outer door opened.

"Forget something, Tina?" she called, stepping around her desk to glance out into the main entrance area where Tina's desk was located.

At the sight of the man in the doorway her breath caught in her throat. No! Not him! It couldn't be!

"Hello, Kendra," Austin Radburn murmured, taking a step inside and closing the door firmly behind him. "It's been a long time."

Bracing herself with one hand on the jamb, Kendra fought to get her heartbeat and quickened breath back under control. She stared at him, hatred surging through her. But that was a good thing, she decided coldly. The hatred was driving out the rush of fear that had caused her palms to go moist. She had spent two years training herself just so she wouldn't react with fear. But perhaps the rational part of her mind had never really expected another encounter with Austin Radburn.

"What do you want, Austin?" she clipped, grateful for the unbelievable steadiness of her voice.

He smiled slowly, and her fear and anger rose another notch. She remembered that smile only too well. Austin's smiles had once been important to her, until she had realized what lay beneath the handsome facade of a face that made women turn their heads to look as Austin passed.

Austin Radburn had been blessed with a thriving business empire and the sun-tanned physique of a man who sailed and played tennis at only the most exclusive clubs. His light-brown hair was styled by one of the most expensive salons in Beverly Hills. He knew how to narrow his vivid blue eyes with a sensual expertise that could make a woman's heart turn over in excitement. And he was capable of a ruthlessness that both Kendra and Donna had discovered the hard way.

Donna had learned that this man was not capable of love; that he could marry a woman for her money, and then nearly drive her to suicide with callousness and unending small cruelties.

But Kendra had learned that Austin Radburn was capable of outright violence.

"What do I want?" he mused, walking toward her with a thin, vicious smile. "Take a guess."

"Donna's not here. You know that by now. She's safe in Lake Tahoe." Kendra's head lifted automatically in silent defiance. She was scared, but she wasn't going to panic.

"Thanks to you, I think," he pointed out, coming to a halt between her and the door. "My sources tell me you were in Lake Tahoe not so long ago yourself. Shortly afterward my dear wife phoned me from there. Quite a coincidence, isn't it?"

Kendra shrugged with exaggerated unconcern. "Think what you like, Austin. She's beyond your reach. And I think you know it or you wouldn't be here, would you?" she added perceptively.

"I could have gotten her and that brat back if it hadn't been for you, my sweet little Kendra," he drawled. "Given a little time I could have made her see sense—"

"Terrorized her into returning, you mean!"

"She always was a weak, helpless little thing. I could make her do anything I wanted—"

"Until you pushed her too far, and she realized just what you *were* doing to her!" Kendra snapped. She had to get out of there. The neighboring offices were deserted by then, and there would be no time to use the phone. Austin Radburn was in a fury. The way he had been that night he'd come to her apartment two years ago.

"She never would have had the courage to run if you hadn't helped her. I finally realized that when it became clear her mother was on my side. I got to thinking about where she could go, who she would get to help her. And then I remembered her charming cousin."

"So you sent Gilbert Phelps to follow me."

"He found you just as you were getting on the plane to Tahoe. He followed you to a casino there and phoned in a report while you were inside. After that I never heard from him again. Strange, isn't it, Kendra? A man dropping out of sight just like that?"

"A pity it hasn't happened to you!" she shot back, forgetting her earlier thoughts about overkill solutions. Donna had been right. It would be pleasant in many respects if Austin Radburn simply faded from the scene.

His eyes narrowed, not with the sensual look he could turn on at will but with a fury she hadn't seen in two years.

"It would seem," he said coldly, "that Donna has effectively removed herself for a while. Sooner or later, though, she'll have to leave her paid protection behind—"

"Paid!" Kendra's astonishment was plain.

"Oh, I understand what she's done," he nodded. "She's bought a bodyguard for herself. I heard all about him in

157

glowing terms. She even told me his name. Wolf. Very impressive, don't you think?"

Donna had claimed Wolf Higgins as her protector? Well, he would make a good one, Kendra felt certain. But she wondered why her cousin hadn't named Case.

"So it would seem I'm going to be out some badly needed money," Austin murmured sadly, gliding forward another step. "But it seems to me I ought to get something out of the deal. You and I have some unfinished business, Kendra. Or have you forgotten?"

Kendra froze, her nails digging into the woodwork of the doorjamb.

"Get out of here, Austin. I have nothing to say to you."

"Good. Because I'm really not interested in a long conversation. I had enough words from you last time, as I recall!"

She read his intentions in his eyes. Austin Radburn had worked himself into a state of violence, and she was once again the intended victim.

But not this time! her mind screamed in cold rage, not this time! She was frightened, but she was in control. She would not surrender to the incipient panic. She had two years of training behind her, and even if that somehow failed, she could fall back on the brutal, deadly little trick Case had shown her.

"Don't touch me, Austin, I'm warning you!"

"Warning me?" he mocked cruelly. "I think you said something like that last time, didn't you? Didn't do you much good, did it? You would be smarter, much smarter, to try being nice to me this time. I was thinking we might go back to your place and get comfortable—"

"You bastard," she hissed. "Do you really think I'm going to let you terrify me into making it *convenient* for you?"

The mockery left his face as he started toward her, his anger in full control of him. "It's all your fault!" he nearly shouted. "All your fault! I needed that money, and you made sure I didn't get it! Well, you're going to pay for helping Donna. And you're going to pay for being too proud to be my mistress two years ago! Just like I made you pay once before! Starting here, tonight! I'm going to watch you plead with me, and when I've listened to all I want to hear, I'm going to take you again and again until you'll do anything I say! Anything! I'm going to break you, Kendra Loring, if it's the last thing I do!"

Kendra didn't waste any more breath in arguing. He was becoming totally irrational, and she had to be prepared for the attack.

It came in the next instant. He swung at her, a huge, backhand swing meant to send her crashing to the carpet with a bleeding mouth.

"You bitch!" he shouted.

CHAPTER TEN

In the end it was almost astonishingly easy. The fear was present, but it didn't hamper her reflexive reaction to the blow. Without even thinking about it Kendra moved, using all the momentum behind Radburn's attack against him.

Her foot slid along the floor as she grasped his sleeve and pulled him even farther into his own swing. She saw the startled look in his furious eyes as she pivoted in a steady, continuous motion that brought her thigh briefly against his. Her left knee slightly bent, she pulled him easily off-balance and against her. Her sweeping right leg caught him with an outward and upward motion just as she released him with her right hand.

Austin Radburn fell heavily to the floor of the office, his breath escaping in a *whooshing* sound.

Kendra didn't hesitate. Even as Radburn groaned heavily and began a violent string of oaths, she was running for the door. She glanced briefly back over her shoulder as she opened it and saw that her assailant was only then trying to get himself off the floor.

She would call the police, she thought wildly. This time there was nothing to stop her. . . .

Her head still half turned to keep an eye on her victim, Kendra didn't see the dark figure in the hall until she collided with him. But she knew who it was even as his arms came out to steady her.

"Case! Oh, Case!" she gasped, lifting her face from his dark jacket to meet his coldly flaring gaze. "It's Radburn! He came to—to—"

She stopped, not because she couldn't say the words, but because the expression on his face told her she didn't need to explain.

"It was him two years ago, wasn't it?" he growled in a soft, deadly voice that sent a chill down her spine. He was holding her tightly, his face drawn and tense, expressing a very dangerous emotion.

"Yes," she whispered, unable to say anything else.

"I finally figured it out on the way down from Tahoe this afternoon." He raised his head to stare at the man behind her, who was scrambling to his feet.

"Get a cab and go home, Kendra," Case continued far too quietly. "I'll take care of everything here—"

"I don't know who the hell you are," Austin bit out behind them, "but this is between me and that bitch. Get out and leave us alone!"

Kendra ignored him, her anxious eyes still on Case's cold, hard face as he stared at Austin Radburn.

"Case, I don't—"

"Go home, Kendra."

He released her, stepping around her and through the doorway, heading toward Austin, who was now on his feet. Kendra whirled and saw the rapid succession of expressions on Austin's features. Something about the deadly purposefulness in Case seemed to be getting through to him.

"Now, see here. This doesn't concern you—"

"No more than disposing of garbage normally concerns me," Case agreed softly. "Still, it's a necessary chore. . . ."

"Who are you?" Austin breathed, and Kendra felt a fierce gladness at the dawning fear in his words. It was time Austin Radburn learned about fear, and she couldn't think of a better instructor for him than Case Garrett.

"I told you," Case murmured. "Just the man who takes out the garbage. Kendra and I have an arrangement. She flattens it, and I get rid of it."

"Are you threatening me?" Austin blustered, backing away from the slowly advancing Case.

"No."

The simplicity of the reply, leaving everything to Austin's imagination, was far more menacing than anything Case could have said. Radburn whitened, and then he turned to glare at Kendra, standing in the doorway.

"Tell him to leave me alone, Kendra. If you let him lay a hand on me, I'll see he goes to jail!"

Kendra looked from his half threatening, half appealing face to Case.

"Case, please don't . . ." she began, her voice still a little shaky from the ordeal.

"Please don't what, Kendra?" Case prompted grimly, not looking at her.

She saw the flicker of relief in Austin's eyes as he decided she was going to call off the dangerous stranger, and she remembered what she had gone through two years ago. And then she thought of what Donna had been through since.

"Please don't leave any evidence, Case," she concluded with chilling satisfaction. Radburn looked stricken.

"Don't worry, honey," Case drawled, still watching Radburn as if the other man were a snake he intended to destroy. "You know me. I'm a professional. No fuss, no mess. I'll see you back at the flat."

"Yes."

Kendra swung around, grabbed her purse out of the closet near the door, and walked out.

She fled into the street, her mind frozen somewhere between the pleasure of revenge and the fear of having tacitly sentenced a man to a horrible fate. She didn't particularly care what happened to Austin Radburn, she realized as she hailed a taxi. But she was terrified that Case might somehow get into trouble.

They had no right to take the law into their own hands, her conscience went on furiously as she sat silently in the back of the taxi. What if the police found out? What if Case were to be arrested for whatever he did to Radburn?

What *would* he do to Radburn? Her mind suddenly shied away from the possibilities as she began to come back to reality. In the heat of the moment back there at the office, she literally hadn't cared if Austin Radburn somehow ceased to exist! God help her!

She should have made Case promise not to do anything . . . anything permanent, she was telling herself by the time the taxi drew up in front of her apartment. She fumbled for cash, chewing on her lower lip in growing agitation. Surely he wouldn't—

So many people knew about Radburn's marriage to Donna. If he was to end up missing, it wouldn't take long before the authorities started asking questions. And the questions would lead them straight to Case, regardless of who he knew or who he could buy. And if he wound up in prison, it would be all her fault!

By the time she inserted the key in her door, she was shaking with an altogether different fear than the one she had known with Austin Radburn. She slammed down her purse and began pacing the Oriental carpet, her mind seething as her imagination supplied endless scenarios that always culminated in Case's arrest. The Radburn family could buy people, too!

She stopped the pacing long enough to brew a cup of tea. Sitting in front of the bay window in the dining room, she tried to think. Case was no fool, he would protect himself. All he'd said, he was a professional. Whatever the hell that meant.

But even professionals made mistakes in the heat of strong emotions, and there was no doubt that where she was concerned he was very emotionally involved. He wanted her. He wanted to take her away with him. What would a man like that do to another man who tried to rape her?

Then she remembered something else. Something Case had said about knowing it was Austin who had attacked her two years ago. Oh, God! If he knew about that . . . !

They had to get out of town. She came to the decision with a thudding realization. Perhaps out of the country. Case was even now doing something she didn't even want to think about. He would cover his tracks well, but in the end the law would figure out what had happened to Austin Radburn.

Kendra made her decision and downed the cup with a clatter. She headed for the bedroom and pulled her suitcase out of the closet.

She was piling expensive French underwear into the bag with reckless disregard for the satin and lace when the security buzzer sounded from the outer door. That would be Case.

She raced to the lock-release button and held it down until she heard the hall door open and close. And then she flung open her door and watched, wide-eyed, as he climbed the stairs toward her.

He looked calm, confident, a little grim, but not the least agitated.

"Are you all right?" she breathed.

He raised one brow sardonically as he came to the top of the stairs and stood looking down at her.

"I'm fine. You're the one who should be asked that question." He reached out and pulled her into his arms with a sudden rough gentleness.

Kendra went into his grasp with a shuddering sigh, and

for a long moment they simply clung together on the landing, neither saying a word. Eventually Case found his voice again. It sounded strangely gritty to Kendra's ears.

"God, Kendra! Why didn't you tell me?" he muttered, his lips in her hair as he held her close. "Why didn't you tell me it was Radburn two years ago?"

"I've never told anyone. In fact, you're the only one who even knows I was raped, let alone that it was Austin Radburn," she confided in a small voice. "How did you figure it out?"

"I finally put two and two together this afternoon," he told her, guiding her into the living room and pulling her down on the white banquette beside him. He cradled her in his arms. "I was talking to Donna about you this morning. Or rather she was talking to me about you," he amended wryly. "She said something about how pleased she was about you and me. She said you hadn't been interested in any man at all for two years. Not since Radburn had abandoned you for her."

"She always felt guilty about that." Kendra shivered.

"When she pointed out that her marriage to Radburn had begun about two years ago and that you'd never seriously dated a man since, I got a terrible premonition. I remembered how certain you had sounded the other night when I asked if you still loved him. I could tell by your voice that you hadn't simply fallen out of love. You hated him. But I figured that was probably because of what he'd later done to Donna."

"He'd been married to Donna a month when he showed up at my apartment one evening." Kendra's voice was low and steady as she told the tale she'd never told anyone. "He'd had a few drinks. He stood in the doorway and started saying terrible things about Donna and how he'd only married her for the money. He wanted me for his mistress and didn't see why we couldn't be lovers."

Case held her more tightly as she trembled at the memories, but he said nothing, letting her tell the story in her own way.

"I told him to go to hell. Suddenly he just—he just erupted through the door. I didn't have time to realize what was happening. He hit me, knocked me to the floor, and then he was overpowering me. Nothing I did seemed to slow him down. He seemed not to feel any of the small pain I managed to inflict with my nails and my teeth."

Kendra broke off, struggling for the words. "The more I struggled, the angrier he got. Eventually he broke a crystal vase, which fell off a nearby table during the fight. He held the jagged edge to my throat and—and raped me."

"Kendra, Kendra," Case soothed, stroking her back with long, comforting movements. "It's all right, sweetheart. You'll never have to worry about him again, I promise you."

She swallowed thickly. "When it was over he left me lying there, straightened his clothes, got in the car, and drove off. I think I was in shock. If you had shown up on my doorstep at that moment with your offer to kill him for me, I would have accepted it without a qualm. Hell, I would have bought you the gun!"

"I wouldn't have used a gun," he rasped. "I would have used my bare hands." There was a pause. "Did you go to the police?"

"I wanted to, but I realized it would be useless. You don't understand, Case. The Radburns are important people. I was a nobody. And I'd been seeing him regularly for a couple of months. Who would believe a tale of rape after that? They would only say I was making it up to get even for his having married Donna. And Donna was the other factor. She was wildly in love with him by then. She thought the world of Austin Radburn. When I tried to talk to her about him, she didn't want to believe anything I said about the inheritance."

"So you kept it bottled inside and started taking lessons so that you would never again be at the mercy of a man like that," Case concluded for her.

"Yes."

"And then I had to come along and destroy all your new self-confidence," he continued, the sudden anger in his voice directed at himself. "I hate to think what you must have gone through this afternoon when you saw him again and no longer had that assurance. I'm so damn sorry to have made you afraid again. If I hadn't done that to you, you wouldn't have had that look in your eyes when you came out the office door."

"I was afraid, but I didn't panic, Case," she told him gently, sensing a need to return the comfort he had been extending to her. "I remembered what you said about panicking. And I remembered that nasty little trick you taught me the other night. I told myself that if worse came to worse, I had that to fall back on. When he came at me everything went perfectly. But I wasn't going to stick around and gloat! Like you said, there's no point welcoming trouble with open arms. I was going to phone the police."

He smiled wryly. "Speaking of the police," he began slowly. "I don't think it will be necessary to—"

"The police!" Kendra sat up abruptly, remembering the urgency of her earlier decision. "Come on, Case, we've got to get moving!" She leaped to her feet, tugging him up beside her and heading for the bedroom.

"Moving where?" he asked reasonably, following as she hurried ahead of him. He stopped in surprise at the sight of the suitcase lying open on the fur bed throw. "What's happening here, honey? Where are you going?"

He swung a curious, cautious look at her as she flew around the room, finishing her packing.

"It's not where *I'm* going, it's where *we're* going!"

"And where might that be? I don't know about you, but

168

personally I'm feeling a little tired. I came back a day early so that we could—"

"There will be plenty of time for rest later," she told him forcefully, slamming down the lid of the suitcase.

"Where?" he asked dryly, folding his arms across his chest and leaning laconically against the jamb.

"On your island!"

"My island!" He straightened at once, staring at her. "What are you talking about?"

"We're leaving for your new hotel as soon as possible," she announced resolutely, glancing around the room for anything else that shouldn't be left behind. She dropped the suitcase on the floor and went to pick up her jewelry case. There were a great many other beautiful things in the room, she thought wistfully, and then she promptly put them out of her mind.

"Are we?" Case asked quietly, his dark gaze seeming to come alive with a new flame.

"Yes, I want you out of town and out of the country. You don't know the Radburns, Case. They've got money and power. They'll find you, no matter how much of the same you have!"

"And your solution is to run?"

"Have you got a better one?" she challenged, moving to stand determinedly in front of him, suitcase and jewelry box in hand. Her brows beetled in a violent little frown. "I don't want you going to jail, Case Garrett!"

"Thank you," he replied feelingly. "But I think I can handle the matter. . . ."

"I know you think you can. That's what's worrying me! You once accused me of being dangerously overconfident, and now you're suffering from the same problem! You simply don't know how much you've bitten off this time by getting rid of Austin Radburn. Let's go!"

She pushed past him, heading for the door.

"Just like this?" he demanded, moving more slowly to

follow her. A shadowed assessment filtered into his expression.

"Of course! The faster we move, the better!" She was already at the door.

"Er, what about the mink coat?" he asked, closing the distance between them with his gliding stride.

She bit her lip, tossing a regretful glance at the hall closet. "I won't be needing it on an island. Leave it."

He raised an eyebrow but said nothing. Instead he walked over and yanked the white fur out of the closet. Tossing it over his arm, he followed her mutely down the stairs. She didn't see the small smile playing around his mouth.

Kendra was already sliding into the black-and-silver Porsche, which waited politely at the curb, when Case reached the sidewalk. She shook her head at sight of the coat but didn't argue.

"We can leave from San Francisco airport," she began as he opened the opposite door. "They're bound to have a flight at least as far as Hawaii. We can make further arrangements from there. I've got a passport—"

"Now you're the one sounding professional," he murmured admiringly, putting the sleek car in gear. "But I think we have a little more time than that. We'll go back to Lake Tahoe first. There are one or two things I should see to before leaving the country."

"Can't Wolf handle them?" she demanded practically.

"He probably could, but since I think we have some time, I'll do it in person. Besides, there's one other thing we can take care of up there without much of a wait."

"What's that?" she asked as he pulled away from the curb.

"Getting married."

"Married!" Her stunned amazement showed as she twisted in the seat to stare at his profile. "You never said anything about marriage!"

170

"What did you think I meant when I asked you to come away with me?" he chided.

"Just that. You said you wanted me. You never said you wanted to marry me!"

Her eyes were glowing when he turned his head briefly to flick her a caressing glance that nearly stopped the breath in her throat.

"I want you. I want you tied to me with every chain I can create. Marriage is one of those chains. Will you marry me, Kendra Loring?"

She put all thoughts of what he had done earlier out of her head. Whatever had happened to Austin Radburn, he'd deserved it!

"Yes, Case," she whispered, "I'll marry you."

"Thank you, Kendra," he said almost formally, his tightening grip on the steering wheel the only evidence of his emotion. "I will try hard to make you happy."

She hesitated and then said very carefully, "There is something you can do for me along those lines, Case . . ."

He said nothing, waiting.

She took a breath and then made the plunge. "I want your word of honor that regardless of what's happened in the past, from now on we will live a—a law-abiding sort of life-style."

He paused and then said very firmly, without inflection, "You have my word on it."

"Thank you, Case." Kendra sank back into the leather seat with a feeling of profound relief.

CHAPTER ELEVEN

"You didn't kill him!"

The thick black lashes of Case's good eye didn't bother to flicker open in response to the accusation. He did shift slightly on the beach towel as his wife paced up and down in front of him, kicking up little arcs of sand with every step. A telegram fluttered in her hand.

"I didn't kill him," he agreed calmly. A tiny smile edged his mouth, a smile that did not go unnoticed by Kendra.

She slued to a halt, her fists on her bikini-encased hips, her hair swaying in a long braid down her back. She glared at his bronzed, near-naked torso and didn't know whether to pour water on him or bury him in the sand.

"You," she declared in ringing accents, "are a scoundrel! A conniving, sneaky, underhanded—"

"You married me thinking I was a lot worse than that. You thought I might easily be a murderer," he pointed out reproachfully, still not opening his eye.

"And you let me think it! My God! When I remember the way you rushed me around in Lake Tahoe two days ago, getting married, making arrangements to fly here to your island, selling the casino to Wolf and Donna . . . !"

"They make a great couple, don't they? Who would have thought the two of them would hit it off so well? After all these years Wolf is settling down to a family life! He told me privately he intends to marry her."

"You needn't sound so self-congratulatory! Donna might very well change her mind before the wedding," Kendra snipped, desperate for any sort of objection. Case Garrett was altogether too confident at the moment.

"Jason would never let her. He idolizes Wolf," Case observed blandly.

"Just the same, Wolf is rushing Donna off her feet, and she might—"

"She loves it. She's finally found a man who can give her the security she needs."

"Hah!"

"I, on the other hand, seem to have married a little shrew. What's all the fuss about? Life will be simpler with that bastard alive, you know. This way we don't have to be afraid to go back to the States to visit Donna and Wolf. No one will come around asking pointed questions, and you don't have to wonder exactly what depths I'm capable of sinking to. What else does Donna say in the telegram?"

Kendra glanced again at the long message. "She says gossip out of L.A. has it that Austin's lawyers have filed for bankruptcy for the shipbuilding business, and that he is staying out of sight while recovering from an 'accident.'"

"You see?" Case offered placatingly. "I didn't let him go scot-free. But if you want to know the truth, what you did to him was far worse."

"What *I* did!" she gasped in amazement. "All I did was throw him once!"

"Do you have any idea what it does to a man like that to have a victim who should have been cowering on her knees handle him as if he were powerless? His ego will never recover. Which was one of the reasons I let him live. Between what we did to him physically and what's happening to him financially, Radburn's a broken man."

"But his family . . ." she began worriedly.

"The shipbuilding business was all the family had left.

174

With it gone, their power is gone, too. Why do you think he was so desperate for Donna's money?"

"Oh."

There was a long pause while Kendra digested that. She narrowed her eyes at his waiting expression. He still hadn't opened his eye to watch her.

"Then, why," she said carefully, "did you let me rush you out of the country? Why didn't you say something when I made you leave San Francisco in such a hurry?"

"I couldn't resist," he admitted, his lashes fluttering open at last as he smiled ruefully up at her. "The opportunity was simply too good to miss. I figured if you knew the full truth and had time to think, it might be weeks before I could talk you into marriage. And who knew how long before you'd agree to leave everything behind in San Francisco and come away with me to this place? So, when you took the bit between your teeth and started to run, I decided it was simplest to just go along for the ride!"

Kendra stared at him, torn between laughter and self-disgust for having let herself be manipulated. But the laughter won out, and it lit her eyes as she said softly, "It probably wouldn't have taken you very long at all to talk me into almost anything," she confided.

It was his turn to stare. "Why not?"

He got to his feet before she could answer, his hands cupping her face as they stood together beneath the brilliant sun, the surf pounding in the background.

"Why wouldn't it have taken very long for me to talk you into coming away with me?" he repeated deeply, something in his voice telling her a great deal depended on her answer.

"Do you have to ask?" she whispered, turning her lips into his palm and kissing him delicately. "I love you, Case. I would have gone anywhere with you," she told him simply.

"Kendra!" he grated, pulling her almost fiercely against

him. "Oh, my darling Kendra. I've wanted so badly to believe that you could be feeling even half of what I'm feeling; that you could return just a tiny portion of the love I have for you!"

She wrapped her arms around his neck, her head sinking down onto his naked shoulder. A great sigh of gratitude shook her.

"You love me, Case? Really love me?"

"More than you'll ever know," he vowed heavily. "I think I fell in love with you the moment I saw you standing in my casino. There was something between us from the first. Did you feel it, my love?"

"I felt it. I had the strangest sensation that I recognized you. I told myself it was impossible; that we'd never met. . . ."

"We're two halves of a whole," he murmured thickly against her hair. "I didn't try to put a name on what I was feeling, I only knew I had to find some way of keeping you with me for a while. I had to find out more about this cool little creature who invaded my casino, intimidated Wolf, and looked down her nose at me. I wanted to make you like me in spite of what you so obviously thought of me! By the time I followed you back to your hotel and found you with Phelps, I had made up my mind—"

"To do what?" Kendra leaned her head back to tease, her hazel eyes glowing with laughter and love.

"To find out everything about you, where you lived, worked, whether there was another man who had a claim on you—"

"And if there had been?"

"Then I would have had to find a way to take you away from him," he told her tersely. "I couldn't just let you walk back out of my life. I thought I had it made when you began seducing me after I'd brought you back from the hotel. When you pulled that judo stunt I was furious. But mostly because I didn't want to believe you had only

176

been leading me on. I wanted to think you were as attracted to me as I was to you."

"I was. But I honestly didn't think about going to bed with you at that point. Sex held no appeal for me."

"I realized that. I also realized I shouldn't have gone ahead and made love to you. I should have given you a lot of time. You'd been through a traumatic experience two years ago, and you were beginning to come out of it on your own. What right did I have to force the process?"

"You didn't force me, you made love to me. And I knew I could have stopped you if I'd wanted to badly enough. But you were something new in my world. Unlike any other man I'd ever met. I knew I was attracted to you, even then. And I was a little stunned from the experience of finding myself first physically and then emotionally vulnerable. I suppose you could say you swept me off my feet. Literally!"

"The process was mutual." He grinned wryly. "Once I'd had you in my bed I knew I wanted you there permanently. I was mad and hurt the next morning when I awoke and found you gone. Nothing on this earth could have stopped me from following you. And you very conveniently left a trail a mile wide!"

"Not intentionally," she muttered ruefully. "I guess I'm not very good at that sort of thing!"

"You were certainly convinced I was." He grinned.

"You didn't go out of your way to convince me otherwise!"

"No, I suppose not. But I didn't think you'd believe me if I loudly proclaimed my innocence."

"And maybe, just maybe, your ego rather relished the idea of making me fall in love with you regardless of my opinion of your—er—profession?" she taunted.

"Well, you had been rather arrogant that first evening in Lake Tahoe—"

"An arrogance that you very effectively nullified!" she accused.

His mouth twisted. "I'm sorry about that, in a way. But I really could see you getting into a lot of trouble coming up against some man who could demolish your defenses in spite of all your fine training!"

"I have come up against just such a man."

"I decided it might as well be me," he admitted. "Besides, I was madder than hell there for a few minutes!"

"I know."

"In one respect I'm glad Radburn showed up again. It gave you a chance to find out you still could take care of yourself. You wouldn't have been a victim that second time. But, then, you never really were. You don't have a victim's mentality. You've got too much courage. You're a fighter, Kendra."

Kendra smiled to herself. Then she thought of something.

"If you're not a wanted man back in the States, we'll be able to go back and get some things from the flat."

"I told Wolf to expect us in a couple of weeks." He chuckled. "He's phoned your partner by now and told him you are on your honeymoon."

"Norris and Tina will think I've lost my marbles." She sighed. "They'll be convinced of it when I offer to sell Norris my share of the business."

His grip tightened. "Is that what you're going to do?"

"Something tells me I'm going to be really terrific at running a hotel for island-hopping tourists," she murmured confidently. "You were right, darling, we can do anything we want together."

"And is this what you want?" he asked, indicating the empty beach and the hotel at the far end; the hotel he had been negotiating to purchase from the present owners.

"Yes," she replied happily. "How did you ever find this place?"

"During the period of my life when you assumed I was apprenticing myself to some underworld lord, I was working a tramp steamer in this part of the world. The man who owned the steamer was the one I told you about that night in the restaurant; the man who became like a father to me. He also owned that casino in Tahoe, and we didn't see a lot of him on the steamer, but occasionally he'd show up and come aboard for a while . . . spend a couple of weeks or months with us in the South Seas—"

"Like when things were a little 'hot' back in the States?"

"You're determined to give me criminal associations, aren't you?" He grinned.

"I don't see you rushing to deny the charges," she retorted cheekily. "Was he a criminal, Case?"

"What he did with his life doesn't affect you and me, honey," Case said smoothly. "He's gone. And he was good to me. The casino was always run legitimately."

She sighed. "Okay, no more questions along that line. But someday I want a lesson in how to break into a flat without leaving a trace."

"Someday I'll give you one," he promised.

"And one in how to make people like Gilbert Phelps disappear."

"Phelps is alive and well as far as I know. But Wolf can be quite intimidating when he chooses."

"Something tells me you can, too. What did you say to Radburn, after you beat him to a pulp, that kept him from going to the police?"

There was a moment's silence above her head.

"Case?"

"Among the other things bequeathed to me by my friend were a number of his contacts. He had some very powerful friends. Their names can make a man like Radburn think twice about taking rash actions."

"Threw your weight around a bit, hmmm?"

"I told him rather succinctly who he might find himself

dealing with if he pushed matters too far. I figured if you believed me capable of certain illegal activities and associations, I could make Radburn believe it, too. And then, of course, I added the clincher."

"Well? Don't leave me in suspense!"

"I told him he wouldn't be long for this world if he ever came near you or Donna again. And that's enough on that subject."

Kendra looked up into his face and knew he spoke the truth. She would not pursue the subject. Instead she smiled.

"I love you so much, Case."

The movement of his hands on her lower back changed subtly, and Kendra smiled with pleasure. Very delicately she closed her teeth into the bare skin of his shoulder. He groaned.

"Vixen," he muttered, fingers digging into her sun-warmed back. "For someone who had, until recently, concluded she didn't like this sort of thing, you've certainly adapted nicely to your wifely duties!"

"I started adapting even before I became a wife, as I recall. You can be very persuasive!"

"Right now I would like to persuade you to take a little walk down the beach and around that cliff with me. There's a very private little lagoon waiting there for us," he suggested in a deep, sexy drawl.

"The other hotel guests don't know about it?"

"I said very private. . . ."

He took her hand, stopping briefly to scoop up the towel and beach bag. Slinging both over his shoulder, Case led her across the sand, around the outcropping, and into a lush, velvet, green place of ferns and trees and incredible flowers.

"It's beautiful," Kendra breathed, absorbing the tropical scene.

"And it's all ours. When we close the deal on the hotel,

we'll keep it that way. Off limits to guests. For owners' use only."

He spread the beach towel on the sandy ground and dropped the beach bag beside it. When he straightened she went into his arms with confidence and love and was rewarded with such a heart-stopping look of need and reciprocated love that she could have wept. Instead she lifted her hands to cup his face and pull him down to her.

"Oh, my love, my life," he sighed against her mouth. "Please, don't ever stop loving me. I couldn't bear it if you were to ever change your mind. . . ."

"Never," she vowed in a throaty whisper. "Never in this life. I think I must have walked into that casino looking for you . . ."

"And I was waiting for you," he concluded.

His lips moved warmly, druggingly on hers, and Kendra felt him undo the clasp of her bikini top. A moment later the scrap of material fell to the ground, and his hands slid around her waist and up to rest just beneath the small, delicate weight of her breasts. With tantalizing slowness he lightly scraped his thumbs across the dark area of her nipples. They hardened beneath his touch, and Kendra moaned as the rising desire caught her.

"So soft and perfect," he rasped, bending his head to kiss first one breast and then the other, his tongue curling hungrily around each thrusting peak.

"Oh, Case . . ."

She stroked his back and waist, her fingers sliding inside the waistband of the small swimming trunks he wore.

"Already I want you so much," she moaned into his mouth. "How do you do this to me?" She peeled the trunks off entirely, molding his muscular buttocks with probing hands.

"We seem to do it to each other!" Gently he picked her up and settled her on the towel, kneeling beside her to drop a string of kisses along the line of her throat, over her breasts, and into the tiny pit of her stomach.

He skimmed off the bikini bottom with both hands and continued the warm, lazy, seductive kisses, following the path of the receding bikini.

Kendra gasped, her fingers tightening convulsively in his thick black hair. She arched herself against his touch again and again. But with maddening deliberation he continued to kiss her while he traced a dizzying pattern all along the inside of her leg, up to her inner thigh.

She began to shift restlessly beneath him, calling his name in little panting cries until he guided her hand intimately against him. Longing to please, she touched him with butterfly softness, caressing and exciting him until Case groaned deep in his chest and moved away from her for a moment.

She heard him fumbling with the zipper of the beach bag and smiled wonderingly.

"You take such good care of me," she whispered, turning to look at him.

"There are some gambles even a professional shouldn't take," he growled as he reached into the bag.

Kendra held her breath for an instant and then said hesitantly, "Unless both parties agree to the stakes."

His head swung around, his dark gaze narrowing with a flash of undisguised hope. His hand stilled on the zipper.

"Kendra?" he questioned huskily.

"We still don't know for certain if there are going to be any results from that first night in Tahoe," she reminded him, growing more sure of herself and him by the second.

"And if there are?"

"Would you mind bringing up a child here in paradise?" she whispered.

"Mind!" The word was a muffled explosion. "Kendra, if I thought you could want a child with me . . ."

She gave him her affirmative answer with smiling eyes.

"I think we could make a very interesting baby together," she said softly. "A little black-haired boy, perhaps . . ."

"With his mother's hazel eyes and courage." Case's hand flattened on her stomach in a gesture of love and possession. "Kendra, my darling, I would very much like to create a baby with you and raise him or her here in paradise."

"Then stop messing about with that beach bag and come here. We're not getting any younger, you know." She laughed seductively, reaching for him.

"You're sure?" he pleaded.

"I'm sure."

With a murmur of passion Case lowered himself to her, finding the soft warmth of her with his aching hardness. She thrilled to the masculine strength of him, the exciting roughness of his thighs against hers, the teasing hair of his chest as he crushed her breasts beneath his weight.

She curled around him, enveloping him with a possessive, feminine passion that he surrendered to even as he mastered it. They gave themselves completely to each other.

Kendra moaned his name against his throat as the flames leaped to consume them. She heard him respond with hoarse sounds of male need. Together they succumbed to the perfect bonding, the essence of which had been reaching out to touch every aspect of their lives from the moment their gazes had locked across the casino floor.

"Kendra! My own, my wife!"

A long time later Kendra's lashes fluttered open, and she focused contentedly on the natural green canopy overhead. As if he knew she were awake, Case stirred slightly, tucking her closer into his curving body.

"You'll be happy here?" he asked again.

"I'd be happy anywhere with you, Case," she told him dreamily.

"The reverse holds true for me," he said softly. "If you ever decide you'd rather go back to San Francisco, I'll take you. I want you to be happy. It's the most important thing in the world to me!"

She thought of something. "Now that you know all my secrets, will you miss your mystery lady?"

"No," he chuckled richly. "The mystery was simply something I wanted to solve and get out of the way so I could get on with the business of making you mine."

"I knew I was lost when I started thinking up ways to reform you," Kendra confessed.

"We hardened professional criminal types need a lot of love and attention to keep us on the straight and narrow," he informed her wisely, lowering his head to touch the tip of his tongue to her parted lips in an intimate little caress. Then he moved on to her ear.

"I'll see you get all you need of both," she promised, wrapping her arms around his neck and bringing his willing mouth back to hers.

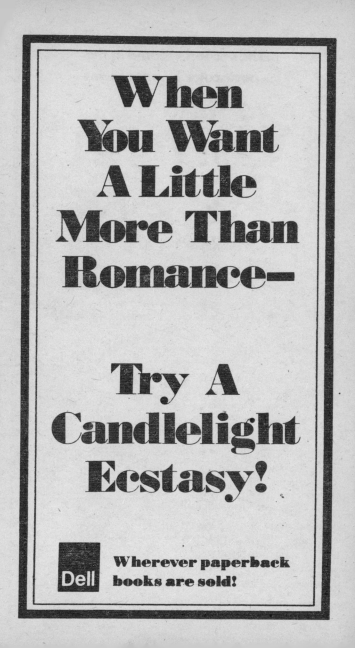

The second volume in the
spectacular Heiress series

The Cornish Heiress

by Roberta Gellis
bestselling author of
The English Heiress

Meg Devoran—by night the flame-haired smuggler, Red Meg.
Hunted and lusted after by many, she was loved by one man
alone...

Philip St. Eyre—his hunger for adventure led him on a
desperate mission into the heart of Napoleon's France.

From midnight trysts in secret smugglers' caves to wild
abandon in enemy lands, they pursued their entwined destinies
to the end—seizing ecstasy, unforgettable adventure—and
love.

A Dell Book   **$3.50**   **(11515-9)**

Danielle Steel

AMERICA'S LEADING LADY OF ROMANCE REIGNS OVER ANOTHER BESTSELLER

A Perfect Stranger

A flawless mix of glamour and love by Danielle Steel, the bestselling author of *The Ring, Palomino* and *Loving*.

A DELL BOOK $3.50   #17221-7

**VOLUME I
IN THE EPIC
NEW SERIES**

*The Morland
Dynasty*

The Founding

by Cynthia Harrod-Eagles

THE FOUNDING, a panoramic saga rich with passion and excitement, launches Dell's most ambitious series to date—THE MORLAND DYNASTY.

From the Wars of the Roses and Tudor England to World War II, THE MORLAND DYNASTY traces the lives, loves and fortunes of a great English family.

A DELL BOOK $3.50   #12677-0

Dell Bestsellers

- [ ] **A PERFECT STRANGER** by Danielle Steel ..$3.50 (17221-7)
- [ ] **FEED YOUR KIDS RIGHT**
  by Lendon Smith, M.D. $3.50 (12706-8)
- [ ] **THE FOUNDING** by Cynthia Harrod-Eagles ..$3.50 (12677-0)
- [ ] **GOODBYE, DARKNESS**
  by William Manchester $3.95 (13110-3)
- [ ] **GENESIS** by W.A. Harbinson $3.50 (12832-3)
- [ ] **FAULT LINES** by James Carroll $3.50 (12436-0)
- [ ] **MORTAL FRIENDS** by James Carroll $3.95 (15790-0)
- [ ] **THE HORN OF AFRICA** by Philip Caputo $3.95 (13675-X)
- [ ] **THE OWLSFANE HORROR** by Duffy Stein ..$3.50 (16781-7)
- [ ] **INGRID BERGMAN: MY STORY**
  by Ingrid Bergman and Alan Burgess $3.95 (14085-4)
- [ ] **THE UNFORGIVEN**
  by Patricia J. MacDonald $3.50 (19123-8)
- [ ] **SOLO** by Jack Higgins $2.95 (18165-8)
- [ ] **THE SOLID GOLD CIRCLE**
  by Sheila Schwartz $3.50 (18156-9)
- [ ] **THE CORNISH HEIRESS**
  by Roberta Gellis $3.50 (11515-9)
- [ ] **THE RING** by Danielle Steel $3.50 (17386-8)
- [ ] **AMERICAN CAESAR**
  by William Manchester $4.50 (10424-6)

At your local bookstore or use this handy coupon for ordering:

DELL BOOKS
P.O. BOX 1000, PINEBROOK, N.J. 07058

Please send me the books I have checked above. I am enclosing $ _____
(please add 75¢ per copy to cover postage and handling). Send check or money
order—no cash or C.O.D.'s. Please allow up to 8 weeks for shipment.

Mr/Mrs/Miss _____

Address _____

City _____ State/Zip _____

Discover the Chinese Wonder Pot!

Ceil Dyer's

WOK COOKERY

Get the most from your wonderful wok! Here's the book that takes the mystery out of wok cookery. Learn to stir-fry, steam, and deep-fry. Discover popular oriental dishes and all-time favorites you can make-in-a-minute. Save time, energy, money— and flavor. You'll wonder why it took this long to discover WOK COOKERY! Over 200 exciting recipes.

Available at your local bookstore or use coupon on last page to order.

$2.95

Dell

A perfect pasta recipe from

PASTA COOKERY...

Quick Vermicelli Soup

4 cups chicken broth
¼ teaspoon dried dill weed
½ teaspoon dried parsley flakes

black pepper to taste
¼ cup broken vermicelli cluster, uncooked

In a 2-quart saucepan bring broth, dill weed, parsley flakes and pepper to a boil. Stir in broken vermicelli. Bring to a boil again. Reduce heat and simmer 4 minutes longer. Serve immediately. Makes 4 servings.

$2.95

Dell